BY STEPHEN BECKER

NOVELS:

The Outcasts (1967)

A Covenant with Death (1965)

Juice (1959)

Shanghai Incident (1955)

The Season of the Stranger (1951)

BIOGRAPHY:

Marshall Field III (1964)

HISTORY:

Comic Art in America (1959)

TRANSLATIONS:

The Town Beyond the Wall (1964)

The Last of the Just (1960)

Someone Will Die Tonight in the Caribbean (1958)

Faraway (1957)

The Sacred Forest (1954)

Mountains in the Desert (1954)

The Colors of the Day (1953)

THE OUTCASTS

STEPHEN BECKER

THE
OUTCASTS

ATHENEUM NEW YORK 1967

To Mary again with more love

THE OUTCASTS

1

Not many go to the ends of the earth for their heart's desire; not many make new ways. Certainly not many men of forty-three cursed by a surly and nervous nature. The last leg of the flight was an agony; they stuttered over sea and jungle beneath indifferent stars, and saw no faintest spark of light or life below. This for endless hours, in an ancient aircraft dragging along behind two archaic propellers. Morrison despised flying. It was unnatural, uncomfortable, and doubtless impossible. He was at the mercy of a pilot, and his life hung on the man's ailments and demons. His fellow passengers enraged him. They were of all human colors but identical in their composure, their silk suits, their plastic pens and important papers, their cuff-links and spectacles and tie-clips and shoes. They were imbecilically calm. The black man beside him read a novel in Dutch while Morrison jittered and twitched. At last he saw lights, first a glow and then clusters pricking out the utter night, and then a pattern of reds and greens and whites that rose to meet them, and tilted away beneath one wing, and rose again; and the aircraft bumped and skidded, earth-

bound. Morrison was immediately exhausted. He was
revived by the metallic voice of the captain, assuring
him that the temperature was ninety-four, that the time
was four-thirty, that there was no fighting either at the
airport or in the capital. Of such consolations is happiness wrought.

On the tarmac he paused. In the night-heat of a country he had never seen, on a continent he had never
trod, panic brushed him. The lights of the runway struggled against the dark immensity, dying abruptly in a final confusion of red and green. The sinister caress of a
hot breeze raised ghosts of failure and sorrow: dead men
in ditches, a woman betrayed, flood, fire, famine, plague.
He retreated quickly toward the terminal building, a
long low wooden shed floating in its own yellow light.
He stumbled; sweat came in a rush, and he went on
more carefully. South America? Possibly Africa? Or
tropical Asia? How could he know? A few degrees off
course. A faulty instrument. The faces (black, brown,
olive) and traces (British, Dutch, French) would be
similar. Wherever you are, keep your papers with you at
all times and do not antagonize the authorities.

Within the shed light glowed through swirls of smoke,
and a dispenser of soft drinks stood like an idol. Languid
bystanders lounged, measuring Morrison without expression. Behind lecterns two officials stamped and nodded
and gestured and smiled. A policeman—white trousers,
blue jacket, blue cap—stood sleepy guard. Moths like
swallows swooped at naked bulbs. The shed was musty,
hot, barny, as though nests of hay were lodged in

shadowed corners, or stolid bullocks ruminating old baggage checks. The two officials wore white uniforms with
brass buttons. Closer, he saw that they wore pistols. Morrison had fought a war but had never worn a pistol. One
of the two took his health card, the other his passport.

"There is no cholera here, you know," the first said.

"I know. But your government suggests the inocula-
tion. In case we pass through choleric regions on the
way."

The man smiled. "That is very good. Choleric regions.
You will find that we have those. Yes, indeed."

The other stamped Morrison's passport, scribbled in-
itials; now Morrison had truly arrived. With many more,
he waited. They were like prisoners, too hot even in their
light suits, shifting and uneasy before the placid, uncaring natives. Natives: he was not to use that word. He
himself was a native of New York State but that was different. Barring a few of the passengers every man in the
shed was black. No. He saw that there were distinctions.
He was standing at a long counter waiting for his bag,
and the customs agents seemed to be Indians. Hindus;
were they called Hindus? How could he know? He knew
that there were many Indians in this country. Some Orientals. Some Portuguese. Englishmen. The signs would
be in English and Dutch and French. That was immediately confirmed by a door that welcomed MEN HEEREN
HOMMES.

They were all too quiet. Only the moths rustled and
fluttered, huge and gray. The men stood, hot and sleepy,
remote one from another and wary, as if none knew

which side the others had taken, or even what the sides were. As if they were waiting for a leader to allot parts and fates: capitalists and communists, satyrs and eunuchs, butterflies and crocodiles. Meanwhile they stood. The policeman yawned a cavernous yawn, and his sigh hummed through the shed; they all looked up at that annunciation, and he brooded back at them with the indifference of authority, a small man, young and weary, above him clouds of cobweb.

The baggage arrived, borne by men and not by wagons. The inspector was listless, with a small nose and a thin mustache. He smelled of cologne. "Any firearms?"

"No."

"Political books or pamphlets?"

"No."

"Occupation?"

"Engineer."

The man nodded, pushed the suitcase at Morrison, and waved him off with both hands, like a farm woman scattering fowl.

A voice stopped Morrison's hand: "Mister Morrison?"

"Yes." The man was very black, Morrison saw, and not noble: a flat nose, thick lips, and the whites of his eyes heavily red. He wore sandals and khaki trousers and a red-and-white sports shirt. He seemed sullen. But then Morrison too felt sullen, hot and thirsty, and what did this man think of him? "Hello. You have a car?"

The man paused in odd astonishment. "Yes. Of course."

"Good. There is just the one bag, here."

After another and longer pause—the man seemed to be memorizing him—Morrison said, "Let's go."

The man altered then, subtly but visibly, and Morrison saw, in the so slight droop of his lids, in the so slight slump of his body, in the so slight fall of his jaw, that the man was mocking him. Ah, spare me pride before dawn! All I want is my hotel. Please, no human credentials. No fraternal assurances. No spiritual negotiations.

"Let's go." His weariness should have been obvious.

"Oh yes," the man said. "Yes, sir. This way, sir," and plucked the bag from the counter in one contemptuous swoop. He was stocky and powerful.

In the far doorway Morrison hesitated. Do you remember coming to a strange city in deep night when you were young, eighteen? Three in the morning, and the streets like black velvet and the gleam of fallen rain like precious stones. And no knowing who watched from which windows, who waited in which doorways; far off a whisper of life, but nearer only the echo of your own steps and the blank gaze of shadowed store-fronts. Until soon it was a dream, and you and your bag were the Wanderer and his Pack, and in the blind windows and blind doorways were ravens and foxes. Yes. Here were no streets and no stores; just a dusty road, a circle of light, half a dozen black men; and for one wrenching moment Morrison was in love with the night.

But he was a hairy creature after all, with too much flesh on him and prey to easy melancholy. He moved grudgingly to the Land-Rover and arranged his graceless limbs and masses in tentative comfort. The man stowed his bag; he moved deliberately and seemed to see nothing; his eyes drooped still, and his face was closed. He wore an expensive wrist-watch, and Morrison thought, restraining scorn, that it was an unwarranted luxury.

"How far to town?"

Again the answer was slow. "Twenty miles, sir." Their lights leapt at the night. The road curved between walls of heavy scrub, and soon there were no lights but their own.

"Good of you to come at this hour," Morrison said.

The man was silent.

"Did you wait long?"

"I had just arrived," he said. "I was a fraction late."

A fraction late. Morrison smiled. "Terrible. I almost had to carry my own bag."

"That would not do at all," the man said.

All right. At five in the morning Morrison did not propose to discriminate finely among tones of voice. The voyage was well begun; that would suffice. No shooting at the airport: an omen. He did not believe in omens but was, as you know, surly and nervous, and far from home. He rocked and swayed with the car. A protuberance of metal hammered at his left knee; he rearranged himself and let his eyes close. The breeze was merely warm now, and soothing. "What's your name?" he asked sleepily.

The silence persisted. Morrison was thinking, a strange one, maybe he hates whites, when the man answered.

"Philips."

For many seconds Morrison merely sat, burning away, a flame in the skin illuminating every pimple and cruelty of his life, every indifference, every theft, every blind murder. To look at the man was impossible. To go back to the baggage counter was impossible. Morrison crumpled, in a weary, familiar resignation; his three Fates, all gums and warts and boils, danced in delight. We hurt or we are hurt, and he could not tell just then which was worse.

"If I were a man of courage I would simply shoot myself," he said. "Fortunately I am a coward, and I have a bridge to build, and I have half an hour or so to make my explanations and frame my apologies."

"None is necessary," said Philips stiffly.

"I'll tell you something," Morrison said, almost too tired, too ruined, to dredge up the words; "that is not for you to decide."

Not many go to the ends of the earth for their heart's desire; not many make new ways. Asked to do both, he had answered in simple outrage: *"Where?"*

The old man told him again.

"With all respect," Morrison said, "you're insane. Cats that eat people. Frogs with hair. Vipers. Malaria."

"Treacherous porters," the old man said with zest. "Chamois bags full of diamonds. Various undignified cruds. The White Goddess."

"I'm forty-three years old."

"I'm seventy-three," Devoe said. "I'd love to go."

Apparently Morrison had giggled.

"What's funny?"

"Everything. Do you know that we are a hundred and seventy-five feet above the earth here and everything in this office is synthetic? We don't even use wooden pencils any more. Your suit's made of coal. Eye of nylon newt. Tongue of polyurethane bat. Styrofoam bosoms." He pressed down on the arms of his chair. "This is naugahyde. What is naugahyde? Does anybody know? Today I shot two naugas. Skinned them out myself. And you want me to go where the hand of man has never set foot."

"Easy now. It's only a job. You don't have to go."

"Oh but I do, I do."

"Easy now," Devoe said again.

Carefully Morrison assembled what composure remained to him after one economic collapse (he was six), one large war (eighteen) and several small (now and then), fifty million dead by violence (here and there), and a marriage for love (on and off). "What is the job?"

"That's better," Devoe said. His voice was even and pleasant, ageless. He had fine white hair and regular features, the smooth bronzed skin of one who had never in his life nicked himself shaving. He emanated clubs and squash, chilled martinis and warmed brandy, horses and small boats and shrill ladies in floppy hats. He was unassailable. In his presence Morrison's own defects were grotesquely exaggerated: lack of breeding, disorderly hair of a muddy reddish color above the mournful features of an aging basset, a fair skin marked by nicks, moles, here a pimple there a comedo. Morrison emanated solitude, divorce, tasteless liquor and fruitless love, floppy ladies in shrill hats. He was assailable.

Devoe droned on, telling Morrison what Morrison knew already. They had bought up a foreign firm and assumed responsibility for a hundred and twenty miles of road, some eighty through jungle and some forty through savanna. Schendel S.A. was the firm, Dutch-British and reputable, cheap labor, cheap materials, and old Schendel gobbling florins and pounds and dollars, pesos and crowns, rials and ticals and yen, regurgitating them into Amsterdam banks like the Dutch East India Company before him, and leaving a rash of roads, docks, skyscrapers, bridges, airports. The offices were in the East Indies and Africa and South America, and now that all those odd little countries were independent, or about to be, and profits were to dip accordingly, and Schendel was growing old, his company was being sold off region by region, job by job. Someone else—Devoe, Sims and Wheeler, for example—would now absorb convertible currencies and defer solemnly to experts in tax avoidance.

All that Morrison knew. "What happened to that other Dutchman? The one who did the work?"

"Van Alstyne. I'm sorry to say that he died last week of a heart attack."

"Sorry."

"I never knew him," Devoe protested. "I know Schendel. A man of quirks. Homosexual, I believe, but in the classic manner of the aging pederast; a collector of butterflies and native art, and not of scruffy sailors. Benevolent and absent-minded. He owned a whole city in Surinam, with swimming pools for the workmen, and a movie and a soccer stadium, and the one time I talked to him he couldn't remember the name of it. He knew Gropius and Maillart. All that. I rather liked him. He's gone back to Europe."

"Who's minding the store?"

"Van Alstyne was, on our job. His assistant is a man named Philips, colored, European education, competent but only thirty. We've half a hundred men working for us there, of assorted colors, religions, and political enthusiasms, and we've a local government to make happy, and we've fallen heir to a good deal of expensive equipment. We're moving in a heavy crane, by the way. I want you there. I want you to finish the job, clean up, maintain the machinery, keep the bureaucrats cheerful, reclaim the performance bonds, see how good Philips is, and keep an eye on the future."

"Why me? All these younger men you have."

Devoe sighed, glittered slightly in his silvery fashion, and smiled the faint crabby smile of the wise elder. "You insist on aging prematurely. That appals me." He went on more gravely. "Much about you is disturbing. You seem to have assumed—well, cosmic burdens to which you have no right. All day long you fret. And I believe I am entitled to hope that truth and justice and the fruit-pickers of California will prevail without usurping the psychic energies of my best field man. You seem haunted by ghosts of your own creation. All right." His elegant hand blessed Morrison and asked silence. "I won't mention that again. But we—the trinity—expect quite a bit of you, and we worry. However," and he brightened, "this is our first job down there, in a land of, um, infinite possibilities. Would you trust Santini, who is so dominated by his senseless and unnecessary struggle to repudiate a background of lasagna and cobbling that he is obsequious to Anglo-Saxons," with a look of wry distaste, "and overbearing to all others? Would you trust Whitman, who chases women and marches on Washington? No. I want you to go. Stable. Almost stodgy. A worrier."

"This begins to sound like a promotion," Morrison said. "I am being groomed."

"As long as it doesn't sound like a raise," Devoe grumbled.

"I'm not like you," Morrison said. "I'm not like you, or Sims or Wheeler. I'm too big for period chairs, and my shirts bunch at the belt. I have no small talk. I went to school in Colorado. I never commanded a destroyer. I was a lousy medical orderly up to my ass in other people's giblets. I worry because they're cutting down all the redwoods to build motels so the contraceptive society will have someplace to go, and putting the Senecas in row housing, and thirty million people starve to death every year."

"Your shirts wouldn't bunch if you wore galluses," Devoe said mildly. "You read too much."

Morrison slumped in his chair, his naugahyde chair. "I don't read at all. The last book I read was Little Women.

What kind of road is this and where does it go to?"

"Crushed rock and earth. To the southern border, or almost."

"To a city? a town?"

"No. Just near the border."

"So where does it end? Up against a wall of trees? With a big sign, fluorescent paint, Now Leaving Our Tropical Paradise, Thank You For Driving Carefully We Love Our Children?"

Devoe sighed again. "Is that our business? We're engineers, builders, not politicians. The road ends at the far edge of an uninhabited plateau, where it slopes down sharply to more jungle. We're not interested in that piece of jungle because they're not sure just where the border lies. Is that satisfactory?"

"Yes, of course. I'm sorry. I wish the world would stop dead for one day. Nobody move. All this constant *doing*. I must be tired."

"You are. As I say, I don't know what loads you force yourself to carry, other than Senecas and redwoods, but the strain shows. However, I can end this conversation on a cheery note."

Morrison waited.

"I'm afraid you'll have to design and build a bridge."

Morrison could only stare.

"Perhaps you could simply copy one of those you have on your wall in there. Sydney Harbor, or Stony Creek. I am correct, am I not, in believing that you have some small interest in bridges? That you worship them in your spare time? When not meditating truth and justice?"

"Is this a joke?"

"Oh, for heaven's sake," Devoe said almost angrily. "Wake up, man."

Well, yes, it was true. Some people have trains, or dachshunds, or fancy paintings, or dirty books. Morrison had bridges. He had always had bridges. Probably he had become an engineer in order to build bridges, but he had never built a bridge, and in drunken moments he saw that as a symbol: his life was a tedious allegory of unbuilt bridges. On the walls of his office, and of his dreary apartment, were photographs and drawings of suspension bridges and arch-span bridges and grass-rope bridges and street bridges, single- double- triple- multiple-arch bridges, viaducts and rolling spans, bascules and swing spans, simple spans and cantilever spans and transporter spans. Steel bridges and iron bridges and concrete bridges and wooden bridges. Brooklyn and the Narrows and Tacoma (before, during, and after), Golden Gate and Stony Creek, Hell Gate and Rainbow, the Landwasser and the Ponte Vecchio and old Sydney Harbor and new Sydney Harbor, and Swiss bridges so slim, so perfect, so daring-young-engineer-on-the-flying-trapeze that their designer had been banished to the untrafficked heights; in their Alpine heaven they soared and floated. There were drawings, sketches, plans, sections of caissons and cofferdams, piers and abutments, roadways and railings. A covered bridge. A pontoon bridge. The Avon at Bath, 1770. Rennie's Waterloo, 1817. The Forth, 1890. Salginatobel, 1930, Rossgraben, 1932, Schwandbach, 1933.

"You told me fifteen years ago—you may not re-member this but I do—that you wanted to build a bridge, any bridge, and now we've got one, and telling you about it gives me enormous pleasure. Here, now, have a drink." From his desk Devoe drew a bottle of malt whisky and two shot-glasses. Attentively, he poured.

Morrison raised the glass with a timid smile."You old fox. You old comedian."

"Don't be impertinent." Devoe grinned. "You'll have to hurry, you know. I have complete surveys and photographs for you. We'll give you all the help you need. Burger can help you with the scaffolding. You have about four months here. Then you go, and the bridge must be finished by October. You'll get heavy rains in October."

"You're going too fast." Morrison sipped at the whisky. "I still think you're joking. You want a Bailey bridge, is that it?"

"My dear Morrison," Devoe said, pained, "you wrong me. You cannot throw a Bailey bridge across a gorge two hundred feet deep."

"How wide is the gap?"

"About twenty-two meters. The bridge is to be about seven meters wide, and is to bear a hundred tons."

"A hundred tons? What for? A million miles from nowhere." But his mind was at work. An old drawing. Yes; twenty meters. Where? Bookcase. Notebook.

"That's what they want. Ours not to reason why. Trucks, I suppose. Tanks. God knows. Defense."

"Defense? Defend what?"

"The border." Devoe shrugged.

"But they don't even know where it is. You said no-body lives there."

"Never mind all that. Just build them a bridge."

"How are the approaches?"

"Flat."

"Geology?"

"Diorite."

"Good. Is there anything across it now?"

Devoe cackled and whooped. "Yes. A rope bridge. Vines. Some nekkid savages on the other side let it down and pull it up when they need it. Won't they be sur-prised."

"Twenty-two meters," he said. "A bridge."

"A bridge," Devoe said. "Designed and built by Ber-nard Morrison."

"Designed and built by Bernard Morrison," Bernard Morrison said.

They rocketed through the night; and yet they were ants, plodding the edge of a shadowy continent. "Help me," he asked Philips. "Make a suggestion."

Soon Philips said, "I suppose it was natural."

"And why was it natural?"

Philips looked at him then, and did not speak.

"Wrong," Morrison said. "At least I hope so. I make no claims for myself, you understand. But when I pic-tured Philips I saw a white linen suit, and a necktie, and a big smile. I had lunch in New York, you know. I've never been here before, or any place like it. Transplanted. Uprooted. Very suddenly. You could have been the prime minister and I wouldn't have known."

"Yes. All right."

"I hope so. Because I don't plan to spend the next six months apologizing."

"Then let it be forgot," Philips said.

Let it be forgot. Sweet and formal tones. Archaic spoken here.

"Where were you trained?"

"Amsterdam and London."

They swooped past a shack; Morrison barely glimpsed advertisements for beer. Ahead, a point of light fluttered, drew nearer; an old man in shorts, on a bicycle, loomed out of the night and dropped behind them.

"I like London. I've never been to Amsterdam. I believe I crossed part of Holland during the war. In a truck, at night."

"You were an engineer then?"

"No. A medical orderly. I wanted to be a doctor."

"And what changed your mind?"

"Blood. They had to send me home because I could no longer look at blood. It isn't easy even now." Beside the road stood many shacks, some on stilts. Before them, flagpoles. Red flags. White flags. "What are those flags? Local communists?"

"No." In the one word was much amusement. "Those are Hindu homes. The flags are religious."

"They keep to the old ways."

"Some. Most are what we call chimár. Backsliders.

Are you religious?"

"No. I could use a drink. Are you?"

"No more. You can drink at the hotel."

"So early?"

"There are no rules. And help, as you have surely
heard, is plentiful and cheap."

"All right now," Morrison said. "Let it be forgot."

Philips smiled.

So they split the night, and shacks and taverns and
crude billboards leapt out of the dark into the cone of
light, like pop-ups in a giant travel folder. Roosters announced them. Goats and donkeys came to stare, wary,
ruby-eyed. Half asleep in the dark wind, Morrison
drooped against his door like a bundle of wash. When
he opened his eyes, he saw that the land was afire.
"What does it mean?"

"They burn it off to clear it."

"Oh. I thought perhaps insect control. Mosquitoes."

"No. It is merely unscientific agriculture. They will
cultivate this land for five years or so and then burn off
another patch."

"Is there fighting around here? Or in town?"

"No. Last week, plenty. I think we will have quiet
now for a while. Some children were killed. One little
girl was decapitated. No one cared to be associated with
that so the leaders went home and deplored loudly, and
after some small looting the trouble was over. For a
time."

"How about the interior? The road. The bridge."

"Nothing. No one cares. In the interior people fight about important matters only, like sacrilege."

"Oh. Good. Are you married?"

"No," Philips said. "And you?"

"Divorced, now. Twice."

Let it be forgot.

"That's not fire," he said a few minutes later.

"No. That is the sun, you see," in a patient, explanatory tone.

Five-fifteen. Morrison quickened. In the faint glow veins of silver streaked the land. The land was quite flat but crisscrossed by silver streaks. "Canals?"

"Irrigation ditches. And drainage ditches. Some are natural. The river is two miles to the east."

The shacks were closer together now. Beyond them, far off, the rain forest, the river, the blood and bones of a continent. In the blush of dawn dark shapes stirred: a naked woman at a well, a man stretching and then slacking to watch them by, his hands dangling and all his weight on one jaunty hip, bowed leg, flat firm foot. Poultry now, pecking at the roadside. A yellow dog also stretched, forelegs flat, tail like a flag.

"Have you been up all night?"

"No. I merely turned out a bit early."

"Thank you. You could have sent someone."

"Protocol," Philips said. "We are a new nation, sensitive to the minor amenities."

"Look at the sun. In five minutes."

"Phœbus' fiery chariot, I believe," Philips said po-

litely. "I see it every morning. By noontime you will not
like it so much. It rushes down in the evening. The
tropics."

Philips went on for a bit about the summer sun in
England, and how late it set, and Morrison listened.
Philips's voice was like music; not a chant, not a sing-
song, but gentle, and with a beat and a warmth to it, and
the almost-British vowels, and no contractions. As
though he loved speaking.

"There are no crops along here," Morrison said.

"No. We are in the suburbs now. These people have
a few chickens and perhaps a goat. They are day work-
ers, unskilled. There are posters at every bus stop urging
them to wear clothes and use forks. The ones with transistor radios are the proletariat. The ones with transistor
radios and tennis shoes are the bourgeoisie."

Morrison laughed, drunk in the golden morning, a
child within him wide-eyed and happy at the sight of
palm trees, gray rotting shacks, red flags and white flags
limp in the hot still air; and more people stirring now,
black, Chinese, Indians. Letting the child play, he imagined that somewhere in this crowded capital were Leb-
anese traders and Portuguese merchants and missionaries
under broad-brimmed black hats; an English ticket-of-
leave man, and an émigré Russian madam and an Irish
mercenary soldier and an earnest management consul-
tant from Cleveland; and a drunken doctor; and perhaps
even his own sloe-eyed half-caste destiny. Good God.

No. It was more than that. It was euphoria. The rap-
ture of the exile. He was responsible for men, and

works, and great sums of money, but he was alone. Alone! And the rain forest and the savanna to swallow him up, if he wanted. Savages, but not as savage as his own kind; cats that ate people, but not one nauga. Fresh running streams, and green mysteries, and a burning sun. He might stay forever. Alone! Free!

Philips blared their way. Dogs and chickens and donkeys—and turkeys!—darted and clopped and fluttered for their lives. A child shouted. Men stared. Women waved. The battered ruin of a bus frayed to a stop, whistling and groaning, and Morrison remembered a story Sims had told: up an Asian river after the war he had passed half an hour in a Buddhist temple before noticing that it was a Liverpool tram. "Low church," he said. Wheeler had driven a 1926 Rolls-Royce in Samarkand, and had eaten twenty-year-old K rations in Cappadocia.

High above them birds wheeled, then drifted lower: graceful, black, commanding, with black-and-white faces and long, slender black wings. "What are they?"

"Carióncru," Philips said.

"Carióncru," Morrison repeated.

Philips smiled. "Very good."

"I don't understand."

"Carrion crow," Philips said distinctly. "We make a different music here."

"Yes. A pretty music."

They swung into a long bow to the left, and Morrison saw a small bridge and a dilapidated factory. There was a bad smell and he looked for dung at the roadside, or a drainage ditch, but saw none, and then it was worse, much worse, and they slogged into it. He gagged. It was the thick, liquid stench of a thousand dead, a world gone to rot, a universe of offal. He gagged again and swallowed, held his breath, groped for a handkerchief. A truck approached. Philips swerved left, off the road, and they jolted to an open patch and came to a halt.

"Not here," Morrison choked. "No."

"Sorry." Philips gestured.

The truck blew past: a weapons-carrier. Half a dozen soldiers stood like statues. They carried short weapons with long, curved magazines. They wore steel helmets and were webbed about with bandoleers. The handkerchief at his mouth was useless. He leaned over the side, but before he could retch they were moving.

"They tend to be rude about the right of way," Philips said. "It is always better to lay by and let them go past."

Morrison looked back, but the dust had obscured them. "The smell," he managed. "What is it?"

Philips pointed to the factory. "That is a molasses refinery. I know. It smells like feces. You will not be able to drink rum for a day or two. But you will grow accustomed to it."

"I hope not. Drive faster, will you?"

"Fifteen hundred people live right here," Philips said blandly. "To them it is merely the air they breathe."

Then it was behind them. Morrison tucked away his handkerchief and noticed with mild surprise that he was wearing a jacket and tie. He removed both and sat back exhausted. He could see tall buildings now, a mile ahead. Six storeys, at any rate. A water-tower. To the right, beyond Philips, a muddy river, coffee-colored in the red-gold morning. Coffee. A shop, the sign in Chinese. A service station, familiar, red white and blue, an American name. Policemen: blue-and-white uniforms, frogging, brass buttons. Bicycles, bicycles everywhere. A shoe store. A pharmacy. The streets were thronged, abruptly, as though men had sprung from the earth, bursting by thousands from the morning's seed. Shirts of white, pink, yellow, red, stripes and checks; dresses of orange and yellow and swirling flowered print; women with hair heaped high, with frizzy hair, with white hair; one in an unadorned white brassiere; a white woman, middle-aged and bespectacled, with a basket of laundry on her head and one graceful arm propping it. Straw hats, cloth hats, flat, crowned, conical. Shirtless men trailing machetes, donkeys yoked in teams, the red dust of the road rising, a mingling of smells now, and the day's heat beginning. A column of foot-soldiers, and the crowd parted in momentary silence. Honey Road Police Station. Librairie Française. The Albert Hotel, ramshackle.

Then a vast open shed, a market, and as they drove slowly past, Morrison saw strange fruits and exotic vegetables, bright yellow and dull red and purple-black. Chickens, live; chickens, dressed. Mounds of nuts and beans. Coffee. Tobacco leaves. An old, old woman, all wrinkles, nearly bald, squatting behind six tomatoes. A heap of coarse yellow flour. Jets of speech, sprays of laughter. Flowing heat. A fat Chinese in madras shorts and a red mandarin hat.

Beyond the market was a traffic circle black with bicycles, and one empty two-ton truck sagging and clank-
ing, billowing and bellowing, leaking dust and exhaust.
They had fallen in lazily behind the truck when the
firing began, and again Philips wrenched the wheel to
the left and ran them off the road, onto the red dust
walk, and they were still jerking to a stop when he
pushed Morrison's head down. "Look later," he said.
They were blind, bent, cramped, heads on their knees,
shoulders touching; they sweated and panted in the
waves of acrid heat and petrol fumes.

"What is it?" Morrison whispered.

"God knows," Philips said in conversational tones.
"We will be all right. We have government license
plates."

"That's grand." Eminent engineer, recently slain,
claims diplomatic immunity.

The first burst had been from machine-guns of some
kind. Then there were single shots. Then a burst again.
There were no shouts, no screams. Trapped and sweating, Morrison remembered a Belgian farmhouse, and the
doctor passing out, slumping forward with a handful of
sponges and lying peacefully in another man's bloody
remains. Then there was another burst and memory fled.
Philips's hand was still on his neck. Scuffling. Shouted
orders. Men at a trot.

A whistle. Philips straightened, slowly. "I think that
is all right now."

Morrison sat up beside him. The traffic circle was

empty. A population had vanished. No troops, no police, no bodies. But immediately the living emerged from doorways. Out of a haberdashery directly in front of them rode a man on a donkey. He was wearing a straw hat with a blue band, and he kicked his mount onto the road and became again a traveler.

"You'd better tell me what's happening," Morrison said.

"No one knows," Philips said.

2

The round black head bobbed like a rotted melon, with sunlight beating off the ashen hair; the body dangled. Not much nose left, two fingers missing; a mismade marionette, even the eyes dulled and uncaring. He hung on one rude crutch at the hotel gate: the porters had not come yet to drive him away. His bad hand begged patiently. He spoke in a language Morrison did not know; but Morrison understood. Morrison could not look away, and for several seconds they stood in the morning light, a rest in the staccato of a wide avenue, breathing the city's brown breath. The black man seemed to focus then; his eyes brightened, and he looked into Morrison's with interest, as though he had waited many days for a man who would not turn away. But Morrison did turn away. He found a small bill and pressed it into that hand, his own fingers crawling and tingling at the touch, and then he turned away, and went back to his room, and washed. When he came out again the man was gone. "There are not many," Philips said later. "There is a small colony on an island offshore but we have few trained people. We need our doctors

and nurses for the healthy. They are almost all white
and with independence many of them left." He
shrugged. "Are there many in America?"

"We have hospitals for them."

"Ah yes. You keep them out of sight."

That was on the third morning. The hotel squatted beside the main avenue between a night club and a com-
mercial building. There were two storeys of it around a
square patio and in the patio was a swimming pool. The
rooms were perfectly anonymous and of no country, im-
placably modern and indistinguishable from rooms in
Paramaribo and Lagos, Jakarta and Manila, Bombay and
Kingston: plaster, tile, fixtures, bureau, desk, air-
conditioner, sterilized tumblers. Prints of exotic flora.
Letterhead stationery: Dear Mother, here I am in Perse-
polis and there is plenty of toilet tissue. Microscopic bars
of gift-wrapped soap. Black plastic ash-trays. We are turtles and not travelers, and all over the world identical
shells await us.

The avenue outside was broad, parted by an esplanade
of grass and flowering shrubbery. In daylight traffic was
ceaseless, bicycles and cars and trucks and dogs: small
smooth-coated hounds of no breed and various muddy
colors. They were everywhere, and they had learned
to move with traffic as their ancestors had moved among
panthers and snakes; they loped carefree among the
wheels, pausing here and there to piss or dung, and they
were often killed, leaving pellets and corpses for the
beetles and scavenger-birds outside department stores,
airlines offices, government ministries and barber shops.

The scavenger-birds were officious and awkward, not carrion crows but much smaller, citified, pecking and ripping and fluttering up in raucous clouds to escape cars and trucks; bicyclists avoided them, veering fastidiously around the maggoty meat. The streets reeked of heat and flesh, flowers and exhaust, dung and the river; on the first day Morrison absorbed the reek, on the second he liked it, on the third he forgot it.

He was in khaki and sneakers by then, his nose and forearms lightly sunburnt. He ignored beggars if not lepers; his education had begun. That first morning they had ordered bacon and eggs at six o'clock, and he had been curious: peccary bacon? bird-of-paradise eggs? A young and very small Indian bellhop whose name was Gordon had taken his bag and shown them to a ground-floor room maintained, in honor of his northern eminence, at a temperature of sixty degrees. His sweat dried like ice in seconds. When he asked Gordon to still the machine, Gordon favored him with a sparkling bow, as though Morrison had complimented the country on its superlative climate. Philips and Morrison returned to the warmth of the morning air and took a table beside the pool. The sun was not yet high enough to brighten the patio, nor was it needed; in ninety-five degrees of heat they sat beside the still waters. "What do we have to do in town, and when do we go to the site?"

"In two or three days," Philips said. "You must buy clothes. Khakis, sandals, a hat, underclothes, and so forth. We will inspect the road on the way out. Although there is not much to be done if you do not approve. You will live in a caravan, as you know, and our field office is also a caravan; a trailer, as you say. They are better than tents. Your blueprints and papers are filed there. The camp is some four miles from the site." He went on. They had thirty men now, most unskilled, some who knew carpentry and concrete, and the best craneman in the country, who had mastered all the heavy machinery available. The men slept in hammocks. Late every Saturday they boarded lorries and were brought to the capital for their weekend.

"And they are brought back on Monday drunk and maimed."

"No," Philips said. "Hung over and maimed."

"Who's the foreman?"

"Ramesh. An Indian, about sixty, very capable. Soft-spoken and always calm, a bit of a philosopher. You may be disturbed by the relatively slow pace. Was that mentioned?"

"No."

"We are in the tropics." Philips shrugged. "You must see it, and feel it. You must keep your temper. You must be patient."

Morrison accepted the "must" provisionally. "This Ramesh: what's his first name?"

"Ramesh is his first name. His last name is Rampersand but everyone calls him Ramesh."

A glistening scarlet butterfly flittered across the blue water and came to rest on a dusty potted palm. A small ginger cat was asleep on the diving-board.

"And we will have dinner soon with a man named

Goray, who is of the government."

But Morrison was too tired, and here came Gordon with their breakfast: ordinary bacon and eggs, except that the bacon was back-bacon and the eggs were over-cooked. The two ate in near-silence, and then Morrison excused himself and slept.

That afternoon they bought his clothes in an arcade, a tunnel through a gloomy office-building, street to street, with squatting venders like malignant mush-rooms, thriving in the cool shadow and bargaining in resigned boredom. The arcade was a haven because the prevailing winds, though they prevailed seldom, swept gently through it. Nothing else swept through it; they waded in empty tin cans, empty cigarette boxes, empty tobacco spills, empty peanut shells, gobs of spittle, broken bottles, poultry feathers, and shards of coconut shell.

Morrison liked the city. He even liked the offices of Schendel S.A., six rooms in a massive Victorian-Dutch-Colonial building with high ceilings and innumerable mysterious stairways. He met his fellow engineers, young graduates who complimented him insistently on his bridge and were rude to their clerks. He examined the books without real interest. He passed judgment on small projects, on blueprints, on renderings, on the lava-tory, which had been refurbished. He had the joy of meeting black men named Isaacson, Utu, and Vieira-Souza. In the office and out he heard many languages, all softly spoken, purling, soothing. They entered him and he too spoke softly, and there was no hurry. He learned that there were six kinds of people: Europeans, blacks, Orientals, Indians, Amerindians and Portuguese, and he wondered what the Portuguese thought about that. Each night at sundown, as they drank on the second-storey terrace and contemplated the avenue and its burdens, its motion, its slaughter, each night at sundown a thin, silvery trill lamented the day, teeee-teeee-teee, from some corner of the ragged shrubbery. "Oh yes," said the Indian waiter. "The six o'clock bee. Not really a bee," he confided. "A bird. Oh my yes. A very small bird."

When the waiter was gone, Philips said, "Oh my yes. Not really a bird either. Oh my no. Really a kind of cricket."

"Why do you make fun of him?"

"I make fun of everybody," Philips said. "In time I will make fun of you."

"That's too easy. Who is Goray, exactly, and should I behave in any special way?"

"Exactly is too much," Philips said. "Approximately is within my powers. Approximately, he is a man in his fifties, very clever and good, and an assistant, or deputy, to the minister of the interior, in whose jurisdiction lie our road and our bridge. Goray and Van Alstyne were friends, and he has taken a great interest in the project."

"Oh." He sensed that Philips knew what he was about to ask. "Am I to understand that he is . . ."

"Is?"

"Is on our payroll?"

Philips leaned back, and because he regretted the need

for the question Morrison dismissed it for the moment
and examined Philips's face, which had altered as he came
to know it better. It was less round than he had thought,
and the cheekbones were stronger; in moments of irrita-
tion there seemed a hidden force, almost a resentful aqui-
linity, like a shadowy skeleton within the flat nose. The
mouth was not simply thick lips; it smiled pleasantly and
unpleasantly, expressed scorn, approval, delight, greed,
pride, faint melancholy.

"Yes," Philips said. "Of course he is on our payroll.
Under 'personnel life and disability insurance,' which we
do not carry. Now first, he is worth three times as much
because he makes unnecessary *any* further contact with
the government. Do you know what a blessing that can
be?"

"I know."

"And second, it is the way of things. Will you object?"

Morrison shook his head slowly and sipped a lovely
cool sip of rum and coconut water. (He had recovered.
In this he was resilient.) "It is also the way of things
in Washington. Graft and nepotism. Have you any
nephews?"

Philips smiled slightly. "But you object, all the same."

"Don't you?"

"No. If I had a nephew, the son of my brother or
sister, would you want me to favor a stranger over him
in the name of efficiency? If so, how far do you carry
the principle? If I had a son who stole, would you want
me to give him to the police? Or a wife who spoke

against the government?"

"I never thought of it that way," Morrison said lazily. It was a marvelous warm evening, and on the river a freighter hooted.

Leaving the hotel, they ambled up the avenue among couples and bunches at their soft evening laughter and gossip. Motor traffic died with the day, and sweeter smells drifted among softer sounds. The street lamps glowed weakly, haloed in moths, and now the buildings were dark, their day's work done; the shops closed at four. The two engineers strolled along the equator in May. On a dark side-street, the smells of cooking, spices; a reclining drunk hummed and keened in a shadowy doorway, and said as they passed, "Good night, sirs," which Morrison knew by then meant "good evening." "Good night," they said. He was reminded of Italians waving good-bye when they meant you to come closer, and vice versa, and he asked Philips if he had seen that. No; but Philips told him how pleasant uninflected pronouns could be, so that "he tell he papa and *he* tell *he* papa" meant son to father to grandfather, and that a house was called a yard, pronounced yod, so that "she has gone home" came out "she go by sh'yod." And here a bastard language had flourished, English-Dutch-local; had Morrison noticed the sticker on their dashboard? Yes; and Philips spoke it: "Lookoe yo oilie nanda watra befosie yo start na wagie." Morrison made him say it again. "But the 'yo' is spelled j-o-e," Philips added. Lookoe joe oilie nanda watra befosie joe start na wagie. Lovely. Morrison

laughed aloud. The warmth was an embrace, the breeze
was a kiss. They passed a squat mosque, a bulbous mina-
ret, and later a cemetery. "That is a Jewish cemetery,"
Philips said. Morrison could see nothing; the stones and
tablets were shapeless and obscure at night. "And so is
that," Philips said in a moment.

"Why two? Are there so many here?"

"One is for the European Jews," Philips said. "I forget
what they are called. The other is for the Sephardic
Jews."

"Segregation everywhere," Morrison said, and Philips
laughed.

Then they were standing before a plain wooden door
with a lantern above it, a single bulb within a cube of
leaded blue and green glass. In black block letters: CHEZ
TAFIAN. When someone nudged his leg, Morrison started
and shied; but it was only a billy-goat, staring up at
him, long of face, bearded, yellow-eyed. Morrison said
"Good night, sir" and the goat's lip curled. With his
horns and yellow eyes and quivering nostrils he reminded
Morrison of something, someone, long ago, mocking and
contemptuous, haughty and unblinking.

Inside he saw no bar, no cashier, only a large room
with almost bare whitewashed walls; in the back screens,
and beyond them a dim garden. Philips led him to a
table and Goray rose to welcome them, a man of aver-
age height but of over two hundred pounds; in his yellow shirt he was a sun. For Morrison he had a bene-
dictory smile and a fat handshake; he bustled. "So! En-

gineer Morrison! Welcome, welcome."

"Thank you." Goray's brilliant smile demanded another. He was very black, and his imposing head sat on a
short neck; a small, upturned nose lent his round face
good humor, possibly because it had to support a large
pair of horn-rimmed spectacles. His hair was graying.
His bare forearms were thick around. So was his belly.
As he sat down, his cane chair creaked softly in anguish.

There were a dozen tables and many other diners, all
men. In one corner, alone, sat a man Morrison took to
be a Portuguese: dark curly hair, hooked nose, mustache.
Goray was still smiling. On each table stood a small
lamp emitting dirty yellow light, and as Morrison made
himself comfortable he was bewildered by the insane
fancy that this was a reunion, that he had been—that
the room itself—the wooden tables—raffia lampshades
—the murmur, the tinkle and clink, the laughter—impossible. Buck up, Morrison. The tropics.

"This is where I always eat," Goray said. "Plain and
good and not expensive. A drink?"

Philips and Morrison took rum and water. Goray ordered a whisky-soda and named his brand. "So. This is
your first time here?"

"Yes."

"And what do you think of our country?"

"It will be the ruin of me."

And it went on like that for some minutes. Behind
him, abruptly, the thrum of a guitar; he turned to see a
troubadour in black trousers and a red shirt picking his
way through the room. He passed their table and went

to a wicker chair, sitting with his back to the screen and smiling a performer's dead smile. He bore, aside from the guitar, what looked like a twelve-ounce tumbler of rum, and his first tune was very sad but crowded with notes.

With their third drink Goray said, "To the bridge. To the bridge. A brilliant bridge. Will it fall down?"

Morrison was shocked, and set down his glass. "Of course not."

"No offense, old man. Tell him about Gimbo while I drink." Goray grinned gleefully and took a long swallow. His fat hands moved swiftly, like a magician's, as Philips spoke, and there appeared as if from nowhere a cigarette case, a lighter, flame, gouts of smoke.

"Gimbo was the first bridge we built after independence," Philips said. There was despair in his tone, but as he went on, it became wistfulness and then amusement. "No problem at all: a narrow river, a brook really, and all we needed was solid abutments and some twelve-meter girders. But we took it quite seriously, and built well. When we were ready for the girders we were all rather excited; I remember the craneman was sweating and shaking. You will meet him. We got the first girder up and swung it out and lowered it gently, slowly, more slowly, no one breathing, and when it was perfectly aligned we lowered it the last bit, and it came down, and down, and down, right through the gap, until it was practically in the water. So we hauled it up and measured the gap, which was just right, and then we measured the girder and it was eleven meters. All of them were." He was smiling now. Goray shook with laughter; his chair creaked. "So we went after the contractor, a Syrian I believe, who had ordered these beams from abroad and wanted us to declare war immediately, because he had bought them from a socialist government and redress would be difficult. This reached our cabinet and we made representations, insulting a sovereign nation. We were preparing a formal protest when Goray had the idea of doing an inventory at the steelyard. The contractor—what was his name?" Goray shrugged happily— "had erected a long shed with posts every few meters marked to separate the different lengths of girder. And he had begun by stacking the girders to the left of the marker, but in time there had been confusion and some were stacked to the right, so everything in the ten-meter bay was nine meters long, and so on. In the thirteen-meter bay were all the twelve-meter girders we could use in a year. So we trucked the short ones back, a hundred and twenty-five miles through the bush, and replaced them, and made a formal apology, and thus averted world war three. Building a bridge is not so simple here."

Goray giggled. "And I was promoted, for my brilliant suggestion. What do you think of that?"

"It's very funny," Morrison said politely.

"And very inefficient and typical of a backward country." Goray smiled still but the mirth was gone away.

"I've seen the phrase in the newspapers," Morrison said slowly. "I never knew it was used in conversation."

"It is better than 'primitive,' " Philips said easily.

"Or 'savage,' " Goray said not so easily.

"I believe the politicians now say 'developing.' " Morrison's tone was light but his hands trembled. "You have no monopoly on mistakes."

Goray glowed, and was lively again. "That is true," he cried. "That is true. The only real democracy. An equality of ineptitude. Well! Now we can eat. Or would you like another?"

They liked another, and drank beer with the meal; Goray ate a stew of lamb and tomatoes, and Philips and Morrison had something called a cook-pot, finely chopped beef with peppers and spices. It required seas of beer. Goray's appetite was as awesome as his good cheer. He chewed and chattered, gestured and bubbled, belched and laughed. He mentioned Erasmus and spoke once in Latin. He talked of the distillation of sea-water and the glories of nuclear power-plants. He said that painting always foreshadowed political change, and told them why, and Morrison did not understand. Morrison swilled and listened. Soon Goray came back to his own country and went on about animism and sculpture. "That you may call primitive," he said. "There it is all right because that is the accepted name for art conceived in the simple and natural spirit. However refined the technique, you see." Morrison did not see, but nodded. "That spirit produced remarkable works, and not merely works of art. My people, for example, had traditional and effective sanitary arrangements when the

English were still defecating in public parks." He chortled. "Did you know that? In public parks. In London. And because it would have been embarrassing to be recognized, they turned their backs to the road. How elegant. The century of your Doctor Johnson. Your Mozart. Your American Revolution. In the public parks." He gobbled his lamb.

Morrison roared laughter, and Goray paused. "You did not know that?" he said. "That strikes you as very funny?"

"No, no," Morrison said, when he could talk. "I was remembering my mother. 'Bernard,' she said, 'there are some things we do not discuss at the table.' "

The guitarist drifted off and came back with a full glass. He was not bothering to smile.

"So they bought tractors," Goray said. They were drinking brandy. The room was hot and full of smoke and music. So was Morrison; also too much food and too much drink. Possibly too much Goray. "All very modern. A revolution in agriculture. Of course they were spending money, which we do not have, for the equivalent of labor, which we have too much of. And then the tractors were used only a few weeks a year." Equivlint of laybah, he said. Few wiks a yah. "And then petrol and oil are expensive. And mechanics are scarce. So the tractors rusted and died. But in isolated spots the harvest went up that year, so the other farmers believed that they could not be better farmers without expensive equipment."

The Portuguese was softly blurred. He was reading a newspaper and smoking a black cigar. The guitarist had tilted his chair against a post and was sitting on the back of his neck.

"Some of them—it goes back a long, long way, before the migrations—knock out two front teeth, upper or lower. Not just a barbaric custom; no. Lockjaw. In case of lockjaw they can still be fed. You must not make the mistake of thinking us primitive."

Morrison looked to Philips for help; Philips avoided his glance. "Developing," Morrison said.

"Ah yes."

It was banana brandy. Goray loved it. Morrison tried to resist but now Philips's eyes warned him.

"You people are afraid of life because you think that happiness demands punishment. So you forestall the fates by taking on the miseries of other people. People that you do not honestly care a fig for. You become crusaders, and annoy everybody."

"Well, I don't know." Morrison was very uncomfortable. His own country, after all. Did he talk about Goray's country that way? No. By God. No. "Anyway that sounds out of date."

"Ah, no. There is a missionary here, one Montgomery . . ."

The Portuguese was gone but the room was still quite smoky. The guitarist was sitting on the floor, and now all his tunes were sad tunes. His woman had run off to Rio. There were no women in the restaurant. Waiters yawned.

"You have been asked to love your neighbor as yourself, which is plainly impossible. All your religions and philosophies ask the impossible. So you feel terrible in public about everything and make speeches about saving other countries from fates worse than death. That way you need not admit that you do not love them at all. Frankly I can think of no fate worse than death."

"I'm just an engineer." Philips would not help him. God damn Philips.

Plink plink. The guitarist lay flat, plinking.

"All right. Just one more. We leave in the morning, you know."

Goray poured.

"You are évolué. You are beyond death. Instead of death you have hospitals and flowers and heaven. Here we still have death. That is why you cannot win your small wars. Because you are fighting people who know death. You refuse to know it."

"I know death," Morrison said. "I have been up to my ass in death." The room had tilted slightly, or perhaps it was his chair. He seemed to be smoking, or at any rate holding, a very bad cigar. "Covered with blood. Amputated arms and legs stacked in a corner."

"Not the same," Goray interrupted.

"I would bloody well like to know why not," Morrison bellowed.

On the bare white ceiling a green lizard flicked his green tail. Plink.

"I don't know what the hell to say to you. Except that you're wrong. A lot of us do care. You seem to know a hell of a lot about a place you've never been to." Morrison knocked over his glass: tinkle, ooze.

The room was almost empty. At one table a waiter slept, gray head pillowed on his crossed arms. Goray was huge. He puffed smoke. The lizard was gone. The horizontal guitarist stared dully toward them; with his thumb he plinkplinkplinked. Morrison rubbed his eyes. "All right," he said. "Just one more." Philips! Philips!

"Unless you admit that you are not more than momentarily perturbed by distant cruelties, you will always be capable of committing them. Until you admit that you do not really weep for Hiroshima, you will make no start on preventing another."

"God-damn right I don't weep for Hiroshima. It saved

ham a mill—half a million lives."

"Nagasaki, then."

"That too."

"They were ready to surrender."

"They why didn't they?"

"You had to forestall the Russians."

"Not me. I was in a hospital in France. And what's wrong with sore—with forestalling the Russians? I don't want to kill people!" Morrison was suddenly shouting; the old waiter stirred. "I hate killing! I never killed anybody and I don't want to kill anybody!"

The guitarist was flat on the floor and apparently unconscious. The room heaved and buckled. Goray swam toward him and away. Morrison was covered with sweat and his own hot fat.

"Well, I know that you would not hesitate to drop one on a colored country. I suppose you might even drop one on a white country. And then enjoy an orgy of self-recrimination."

"You must hate us," Morrison said. Tears rose to his eyes; they brimmed. Ridiculous. "We *did* hesitate. We *do* hesitate. Who's we? *I* hesitate. There. *I* sure God hesitate."

"But who are you?"

Morrison brightened. "Now that's a question I can answer. I am Bernard Morrison, master of civil engineering and acknowledged worrier. Full of banana brandy, and sure of only one thing in life: it is time to go home.

I *know* that. In my blood and my bones I know it. And my belly."

Goray was gone and the night was starry; stars swooped and swam. Morrison's arm was around Philips's shoulders, and when he looked down there was the billy-goat, sneering and yellow-eyed.

"The devil," he said. "That was it. When I was a boy, they told me what the devil looked like, and there he is."

"Just a little he-goat," Philips said soothingly.

"You're a great help. Where were you when I needed you? You let that fat bastard tromp all over me."

"This way," Philips said. "Easy now."

Outside the hotel Morrison shook him off.

"Forty years ago," Philips said, "they hanged his father for political reasons."

3

Then was his head puffed up and his heart minished, an ague upon him and his very corpuscles reeking banana. Philips woke him at five; he thrashed his way reluctantly to the surface of his shame, and masked the shame in groans and grumbles, and sat on the bed rocking and keening like a crone bereaved. *"This* is primitive. Barbarous. Undeveloped. Waking a sick man at five in the morning."

"Take a shower," Philips said. "I will order breakfast."

"Coffee. Just coffee. Forgive me. This is terrible."

"New lands, new drinks," Philips said. "A shower. Brush your teeth."

"Yes."

"It was that brandy," Philips said. "We drank two bottles."

"And you drank almost none."

Philips smiled faintly. "And I drank almost none. I rarely drink much. When I do, you will know it. I fight and shout, and the next day I lie dying all day long. No one has a monopoly on mistakes, as I believe you stated last night."

Morrison noticed, squinting and blinking, that the whites of Philips's eyes were clear, and seemed to remember that they had been clear after that first morning. "Had you been drinking the night before I got here?"

"Yes. And then up at three to do my duty."

"God." Morrison shuddered, truly: his body quivered. "Sorry. If you felt anything like this you must have hated me."

Philips made no answer.

"Did I insult Goray?"

"No," Philips said shortly. "Goray likes you."

"Then he is a man of great tolerance and easy affections. I was shouting at one point."

"You were shouting at several points. Shouting is normal and natural, and better than brawling."

"Brawling." Morrison winced. Worse than a tourist. "All right. Ready in a minute. But drive carefully, please. I am not a well man."

"You will be well. As soon as we are out of the city."

He meant more than that: it was an incantation, a prophecy, and his low voice and grave face were the voice and face of a pagan priest, who had talked with the sun and the river.

He had built a good road, poor dead Van Alstyne: left that much behind him, not the ordinary tropical rut, and it would endure. His immortality, as the bridge might be Morrison's. Beneath them was hard rolled rock, and broken stone, and a layer of crushed rock and stone, and then red earth, clayey and cohesive so that

the dust behind them was a thin pink plume and not a
gassy billow. Every fifty meters a narrow slash ran
obliquely from the gutter to a sump in the brush. That
seemed a nicety, and Morrison questioned it. "The rains
are of an extraordinary violence," Philips insisted.

The jungle, close on either hand, skimmed by at fifty
miles an hour. Morrison searched and peered, for what
mysteries he could not have said: snakes perhaps, or
savages, a sign of flesh or habitation. But there was nothing, only the green that so close was not even lush: beneath the canopy of palm and broadleaf were no tangled
lianas or profusion of fronds, only some dry and dusty
vines and stunted shrubs, and great hollows of shade.
He had expected underbrush, thick and wild and steaming, wild pigs, lizards, monkeys. Later there were slashes
in the jungle and he did see a hut, but no smoke, no motion. Only the shadowed green, and the brass-bright sun
in a dazzling blue sky, and the road Roman-red, and
nothing alive but themselves and the carrion crows.
The colors pulsed, and he shut his eyes against them.

"Nothing," Philips said. "But later there will be
farms here. Timbering. Stores. Taverns."

"Taverns. Faugh."

"Feeling better?"

"A little."

"We need those farms," Philips said. "Goray was saying last night that it was impossible to starve to death
here, with the mangoes and cassava and coconuts and so
forth. But it is possible to be undernourished with a full
belly. We need cattle, and along here will be ranches

too. We want to bring in zebus from the Portagee side."

"Must we talk about food?"

"Yes," Philips said amiably. "When I was in mission school the white children laughed and played all day long; but even before the noonday meal the black children were played out. Exhausted. When you see the men working very slowly, remember that they have had little protein in all their lives."

"I will. How did you get to mission school?"

"I was an orphan, from God knows where, and was arrested at seven for pilferage. I was stealing eggs from the father's chickens. He took pity on me and let me stay, and taught me letters. He was unctuous and I hated him. It took me twenty years to learn gratitude."

"Where was that?"

"On the coast, where there is a breeze and where the Europeans live."

"Oh. What are zebus?"

"Brahman cattle, you call them. All we have now are scrub cattle."

They were quiet then, as the sun climbed higher. In the solitude Morrison grew anxious—not quite fear, yet not much different—but then the disquiet was laid by the heat, by a lazy abandon, by the shifting colors and the rush of the road. This desolation was at worst neutral. The spirits, if any, would emerge by night, and by then he would have company and a lamp and—the thought was just tolerable now—a drink. And there was beauty here. Nature in masses was always beautiful: seas and forests, glaciers, fields of snow, deserts, cloudbursts, hurricanes. Man in masses was never beautiful, and he remembered for a moment, but only for a moment, the shrill, writhing northern city he had left, and the gray winter he had survived, with snow that was slush even before it touched the asphalt. Remote now; more remote with every mile. Time and space annihilated. What no longer exists has never existed. Here and now only. He slumped lower and shut his eyes again, and sniffed at the warm wind. Soon he was asleep.

He awoke parched and sweating and saw that the road was no longer flat. They were rising slowly, and the jungle had thinned. Far ahead were patches of treeless upland dotted with white. To the east, the blue flash of a stream. He found the canteen and drank, and offered it to Philips, who also drank. "How long did I sleep?"

"Half an hour."

Morrison concentrated on the white dots. They were probably boulders. There was a good warmth in his chest and along his shoulders, and he could feel the strength in his arms. Philips had good arms. They were black and hairless. Morrison's were fair and freckled with a curly crop of fine reddish hair.

"Put on a hat now," Philips said. "We make our own wind and it is deceptive. The sun is dangerous."

Morrison fished the jockey cap from his hip pocket. Bright purple, silky in the sun. Of all colors he liked best purples and oranges. A newspaper had once told him that a preference for orange indicated a cheerful

personality. A preference for purple indicated a melancholy personality. On the same page were astrological
revelations, and he learned that this was a good time to
take the wife on a voyage of pleasure. It was the day of
his first divorce. Final decree. Joanne. Eminent lover re-
calls early transports. God!

He wondered again what life this country bred, and
when he would see it. This upland was not a plateau but
a range of low hills, not even hills, gentle scallops one
after another so that the road had no need to curve but
rose gently with them. The palms and broadleaf had
thinned at the road's edge, and wild patches of tawny
grass, short and bristly, grew there like sideburns. The
sky was lighter but still dazzling, a painter's yellow sky.
In one clearing he saw a white dot much closer, and it
was not a boulder but a termites' hill, pale gray, papery,
like a wasps' nest four feet high and crested. There were
hundreds of them.

Still they rose, and soon the road curved gently, and
curved again, and again and again in a soothing al-
ternation. Before them were green hills, with nests of
purple shade, and reddish outcroppings, and soon they
were rising again. Then he saw the carrion crows, fifteen
or twenty of them, high and circling, remote and patient.
He had missed them. They were good company.

At first he saw only one man, just this side of a bend.
For three hours he had seen no human being: this was
the first. The man was still, leaning on a tamp. He was
tall, black, thin, barefoot, in a pair of tattered pants, and
weary; he raised the tamp in salute, as if witnessing

man's bondage to tools and to work, as if he ate nor slept nor loved, lived nor died, but only tamped. As they rumbled by, Philips waved, and the man waved back, and Morrison saw that he had lost one eye.

Then Philips pressed the horn, one long blast, and they were home, sweeping around the last bend. The crew was startled into a Greek immobility, and stood like a frieze in the spanking sunlight: the digger, the chopper, the sifter, the tamper, the pounder, the roller, shovel and basket, pick and barrow, tall men and round, clothed men and naked, hats and caps and one beret and one scarlet fez.

Then they moved, downed tools and swarmed toward the car, and Morrison saw the roadbed beyond them, the wide swath through trees and grass, still rising pale and dusty, steeper here; and closer he saw three small trailers and a steamshovel and a steamroller and a back-hoe, all off the road and in the shade, and three ancient trucks powdered and gray. And a donkey and chickens and a grinning brown dog. And a blue butterfly darting.

He stepped out of the Land-Rover and stretched beneath the molten sun, and was happier than he had ever been before.

"This is Ramesh," Philips said. "Mister Bernard Morrison."

Ramesh was surely sixty, slight and wiry, barefoot. His khaki shirt was fresh and carefully buttoned, which marked him, Morrison supposed, as foreman. That, and the great silvery wrist-watch with its complication of

dials and sweeps. Ramesh had a large nose and large
ears, sleepy liquid brown eyes and long black hair salted
gray. He was a shade less dark than Philips. Palms together, he bowed, and then held forth his right hand.
"Mister Morrison," he said softly. "Welcome to the
works. I hope you have approved of the road." His
voice was like his eyes, deep and liquid and sleepy.

"I have. The men must have worked well."

"Yes. It took almost two years." His tone was judicious,
as though he were considering for the first time the
quality of his men's work. "Mister Van Alstyne left
them to me, you see. We lost only one. He fell off the
lorry on a Saturday night, going to the capital, and broke
his head. They work well because the job here is a good
one to have. There are many unemployed, as you
know."

"Yes."

"That is because the big city attracts so many, but
we have no money for capital expenditures, for great
projects. Yet no one now wishes to farm. Only my own
people, who are more industrious than most. The sense
of exile, you understand. In the big city there is not suffi-
cient work, and most of the newcomers become a bur-
den to their relatives, who cannot turn them away. We
have great troubles, as you know."

"Mister Morrison needs rest," Philips said lightly. "I
think you can tell him later about our history and geog-
raphy and economics."

"Yes, yes. You must forgive me." They walked toward the trailers. The crew had been shown their new

boss, and nodded and waved now and melted into the shade. The man in the scarlet fez, a giant, stood longer than the others and stared at Morrison.

"Where do they sleep?"

Ramesh waved carelessly. "Back under the trees we have hammocks. Also the cooking truck. Are you hungry?"

"No. Thirsty."

"Ah, yes. Here we are. This is your home and office, Mister Morrison."

At first he could see nothing; after the glare of the road his home-and-office was a lightless cave. Then he made out a bed, cabinets, a hinged desk-top. "Fine. Hot, though."

"Yes," Philips said. "An oven, I am afraid."

"Damn and blahst," Ramesh said in obvious excitement. "Wait," and left them.

"I hope I can sleep in this thing. Let's get out."

"Yes. By noontime the temperature will rise to about one hundred and ten degrees."

Morrison grimaced. "Is there a stream?"

"A quarter-mile off. Down that slope."

"Good. We can wallow."

"Yes. We all do. Um: I have a suggestion." Philips scratched his head, smiling, promising mischief.

"Make it."

"Would you like a bottle of beer?"

"Yes."

"Four hours ago you took the pledge."

"Beer is medicine. Where do you keep it?"

"Well, we have a generator. So we have a small fridge."

Ramesh scuttled up. "Here you are, sir. Welcome." He handed Morrison a broad straw fan with a three-inch fringe of whiskers. Horsehair. "The fan will cool you. The hairs are to whisk flies. Welcome, welcome." He stepped back and made a leg like the Lord Mayor of London.

"The flies can be bad," Philips said. "We call them lion flies. They raise great welts that itch fiercely. We also have insect repellent."

"Do they . . ." Morrison hesitated, and then met his eye: "Do they bother everybody?"

"They bother all men alike," Philips said coldly.

Ramesh seemed puzzled.

"Time for a beer," Morrison said.

"Two a day, only," Philips said.

"All men alike?"

"No," Philips said flatly. "Officers only."

Morrison smiled at him, and Philips looked away.

When the sun was high and cruel, the crew surrendered. They came in a slow snickering hubbub and stacked their tools, and drifted into the dark woods, their voices velvety. The dog, the donkey, and several chickens shared torpid peace in one patch of shade; the chickens twitched uneasily, staring out at the ring of brightness. Morrison yawned and stretched. "Why don't these animals go to the water?"

"Because they are fed here," Philips said. "No need to

have them dunging along the banks. The dogs and don-key go by themselves to drink, and always come back to this spot. What the chickens do I am not sure. They seem to be teetotalers."

"Do they lay eggs?"

"Of course. One egg per man every third day. Small eggs."

"And nothing comes to kill them." He was fighting to keep awake.

"Not so far. Not here. Back in the lowlands we kept no chickens because there are mongooses. Chiefly in the sugar cane but also in the bush. But not here."

"Mongooses." That pleased him. "What about snakes? And what about the big cats?"

Philips dismissed his exotic fantasies. "No. Here and there a viper, more afraid of you than you are of him. Though they can kill. Constrictors taste like chicken, by the way. And back where the forest and the savanna meet there are a few cats. They eat the wild pigs and the dwarf deer. But here it is too open. They are not like those haughty African lions you read about; no, these are something else. They live in pairs and not in prides. They are mangy and sullen and keep to them-selves. At any rate they never come here. And see who is lecturing on the fauna." With a droll face. "Former egg-thief. Now professional man and city-dweller."

"Do you keep arms here?" The men had scattered down many faint tracks through the forest; they fol-lowed along. Hammocks hung limp among the trees. The beer had lulled Morrison and last night was remote. The crowded city and the foolish arguments were remote. Philips and he stepped slowly; even in shadow the heat was thick and sticky.

"A couple of rifles and a revolver. So far not used. I suppose a cat might come. An old one, an outcast."

"I thought you might hunt your own meat." A tangle of roots thick as your arm. Then a clearing of dry yellow grass crackling underfoot, and the sun like a hammer.

"No. If something came along I suppose we would shoot it. But nothing comes along. Animals do not like men. And we have no time to go chasing them."

There was the water, a friendly and easygoing river, light green with scales of gold. Dappled and spangled, purling and licking. Twenty feet wide, and gliding sixty or seventy feet from one bend to another. Its banks were overgrown by heavy brush, leafy and dense like stunted alders, shady. In a copse on the near bank stood a half-ton truck, and beside it a grill about six feet square. "You burn wood."

Philips laughed, short, scornful: "No. Gas. From a tank on the lorry there. All very civilized. But at midday we eat cold meat and biscuits. The stream is clean, by the way. Potable. Go downstream to relieve yourself."

Which some of the men were doing. Most were sitting along the banks waist-deep. Some were naked, some in shorts. There was the one in his red fez, a huge man and wearing only the fez. Morrison trailed after Philips to the cold grill and took up a tin mess kit. Ramesh bowed like a head waiter and indicated a small vat. Morrison spooned cold lamb and took biscuits from a tall can. Sweat ran down his arms. "Breakfast is the best," Ramesh fluttered. "Hot meat and good coffee, made by me, the best, and sometimes cold tomatoes from a tin. In a week you will hate the food. Oh yes. If not sooner. We all do." Cheerfully.

Philips and Morrison sat upon the ground. Ramesh joined them and was silent. They were in shade but the air was like wool. Breathing was not easy, and the food was dry and tasteless. Morrison went to the stream and drank from cupped hands. The men were lined beneath the banks now like a guard of honor, dull of eye and inert, save a few cleaning their kits with mud. A very young fellow collected the kits and carried them to the truck, making many trips and glancing skittishly at Morrison as he passed. "That is Jacob," Ramesh said softly. Jacob wore khaki shorts and a cloth cap like the homespun caps of India. He was black, and gleamed. He waited at the truck, and when the three men had eaten he took their kits. Philips led Morrison to the stream and they stripped and stepped into the cool water, and then to a small cove where half a dozen fat rocks, stippled gray and white, broke the surface. There they sat, and leaned back against the rocks, and were cool and sleepy. The stream lapped at Morrison's belly. High above, the carrion crows planed, and the sun flashed off their white faces. "No one talks," Morrison said.

"About what?" Philips spoke lazily and wanted no answer. Morrison rolled forward, went under, and swam a few strokes.

"Lord Greystoke," Philips said.

"Who?"

"Tarzan."

Morrison laughed and sat back. A blue butterfly, and then another, piercing, luminescent blue, skittered along the glinting waters. Morrison drank again; the water was sweet, and warm to the mouth, but a blessing on the skin.

After a time he was restless. "I'm going on up."

"What for?"

"I don't know. Look around. Guard the trucks."

Philips smiled sleepily. "There is no one. For miles and miles."

"It's too new. I can't sit still."

"All right. While I think of it, if you are ever lost, move east. Sooner or later you will find this stream."

"It's only a quarter of a mile."

"Now or later," Philips said.

Morrison's kingdom. A harsh, bare, flat, dusty roadbed, and the slopes beyond, and the rash of termite hills. Patches of dry, leafy forest, black and silver and a haze of dark green. Three trailers, six trucks in all, the bulldozer, the roller. The machinery was clean and well greased. Drums of petrol. Three days, and he thought of it as petrol. Lookoe joe oilie nanda watra. Spark plugs. Filters. Dynamite. The generator, silent on a caisson; wires. Power. A surveyor's rod.

A junkyard. Plus men, equaled miles of road. Where nothing had been.

He walked out upon the crushed rock; then slower, as

the heat bore him down; then stood, bathed in gold.
Alone. Above him the sun, and below him his own
road. The silence of noon.

A king. A silly man in a silly purple hat.

First man back was the big fellow with the red fez.
By then Morrison was sitting sensibly in the doorway
of his trailer, and fanning. Shorts and sandals and a fan,
and the flies be damned. Welts. The big man came quietly up one of the faint tracks, and the first Morrison
knew of him was a barrel voice intoning, "Hello, new
boss."

Morrison stilled the fan. "Hello. What are you
called?"

"Tall Boy," he said. He was that. Six feet six inches
and an eighth of a ton. An open and amiable face,
roundish, and the fez sitting cocky and scarlet.

"They call me Morrison."

Tall Boy nodded as though this was important in-
formation. It might be just that. In some parts of the
world names were of the first importance.

"What work do you do?"

Tall Boy squatted on his heels. "I move the earth."

He could have, too. Archimedes: give me a Tall Boy
tall enough.

"Any machine you have, I can run." It rolled out of
him like poetry: *an*-y *mah*-shin *you*-hov *I*-con *rawn*.

"Then you're the craneman."

"Oh yes. I run the cranes too."

"I heard you were the best craneman in the country."

A grin. "You heard that."

"Yes."

"That is true. I know where you heard that, and it is true."

"Good. You know we will have a new crane. The biggest and best. Fifty tons, and with a boom that we can run out about a hundred and fifty feet."

"Ah." He gleamed.

"With a full-circle swing. And it can lift thirty-three thousand pounds if it has to."

"Ooo." Moon-eyed.

"You and I and Philips will get to know it before we put it to work. It costs a hundred thousand dollars, and it's all yours."

"Lord Jesus," he said. He was a big man and the crane was right for him. A jockey could operate it, but Tall Boy and the crane would be a love affair. He seemed to speak with great solemnity, but perhaps it was only the deep voice. "I saw a picture of the bridge. Philips told me about the work."

"Good."

They were silent for a time. Tall Boy was noticing Morrison: the flabby belly and the pale freckled skin.

"Boss," he said.

"What?"

"How come Philips is not boss?"

"You don't like me?"

"Oh nothing like that. But Philips did all this job with Mister Van. A good road." Tall Boy pouted and cocked his head like a black pigeon.

"I'm older," Morrison said. "I've done much more of this work."

"Many bridges?"

"No. No bridges."

"Well then."

"There are many men in the company," Morrison said, "and millions of dollars to spend. There is more to a bridge than just the building. So Philips is your boss if you want. But I have to be Philips's boss. In ten years Philips can be top man. You understand. Your own prime minister wants me here." He was not sure of that but it sounded imposing.

"All right." Tall Boy squatted, huge and black and worried.

"No. Tell me: do you understand?" Morrison was suddenly gloomy with the importance of this.

"Yes. You are the boss of the company. Philips is the boss of the work and Ramesh is the boss of the men. I boss the machines."

"Good. And don't talk about this. You shouldn't have talked to me about it. You make me think that Philips is unhappy and wants to be boss."

"Well," he said.

"Don't talk about it again, you hear?"

"I hear."

Other voices: the men returning.

"Philips is a good man. The best. Only young. Everything in time."

"All right."

"And the important thing is the bridge."

"Yes."

Philips was ambling toward them. Ramesh too. "Tall Boy," Ramesh called.

"Ho," he said.

"Back to the road."

Philips watched him go. "That is a good man."

"Yes." Morrison plunged ahead, not sure that he should, but helpless. "He wishes you were boss here."

"He is a simple fellow," Philips said.

"Do you wish it too?"

Ramesh stood wide-eyed, avid.

"No," Philips said easily. "When Van Alstyne died, the men assumed that I was crown prince. I am sorry if Tall Boy has made you nervous. That is the truth."

"Good. What's his real name?"

"I have no idea. Ramesh?"

Ramesh shook his head. "Just Tall Boy. Only Tall Boy. His friends call him Tallie."

Morrison grunted.

Philips showed puzzlement.

Morrison sighed. "In my country, you see, it would be disrespectful."

"Oh yes." Philips had it now. "As with waiters and porters and such. Well, that way we do not care for it either. But when it is a man's name. You worry too much."

"Senecas and redwoods."

"What?"

"Nothing." He rose, and tossed the fan into the trailer. "I'm going up to the gorge."

"Good." Philips beamed. "I will show you the way."

"No. Not the first time. I want to see it alone. Just tell me."

Philips shrugged, turning away. "Follow the roadbed."

He was offended. Ramesh was still wide-eyed. To hell with both of them. And Tall Boy too. It's my bridge.

He slithered and crunched over the shiny, fist-sized rock. Soon the grass at the road's edge invited easier walking. It was coarse and tough. After a mile or so it became denser and deeper, and he heard an echo of Philips, "here and there a viper," and moved back onto the roadbed. Which then became a simple track, rising with the land. Still the trees were sparse, still the sun merciless, but before him was a new terrain, purple and gold and black, with hills and hollows, and far off to his left—he was marching south, so that would be east —a range of real mountains. And still the road rose.

On that hour's journey he never looked back.

In the end he followed the track through a last grove of stunted upland broadleafs, and paused once, weary, grateful for the shade. In the silence he heard a woodpecker—never saw it—and the rattle took him back thirty years. He was a boy again, and a country boy too, and the sweat on his round face matted a fine down. He was lost in the woods, and happy. Jacknife in his pocket and all things still to come.

The canopy of leaves was tightly woven, passing no blue and no sun. He stood on the musty forest floor in a cave of feeble greens and grays among black roots and trunks. Behind him a light crackle; he turned to peer, as if stalking beasts padded in shadow. Nothing. The spirit of the place. The souls of lions and vipers, but no bodies; only yellow eyes, lidded, winking behind tree-trunks.

A small boy, and all things still to come. Chirr. Kee-kee-kee. A flash of yellow, high in the leaves.

All sad things. He moved along, through school and war and wives and work, and his round face grew long, and the fine down thickened and bristled, and the clear eyes veined slowly red. He came out of the grove through a forlorn hope of gallant red blossoms. They were low to the ground and huddled against the sunlight.

He stood small in a great bowl of yellowed grasses, dwarfed by the dappled hills and the raw blue sky. It was a cracked bowl, and the crack was his gorge, a hundred steps on. The gorge emerged from steep hills to the east, dirty yellow hills with a blush of reddish brown, and black rocks nippling up; beyond those hills were the mountains he could no longer see. But to the west the hills sloped away, and were a rich green, and stopped his breath: a million miles of rolling green, hill and forest, palm and broadleaf forever and a hair of blue, a river, another; the sun westering now but still sovereign, blinding, and the green beneath endless, flashing bright, shadowed dim.

Alone. Oh, he was alone.

His saucer was a small flat circle, a resting-place in the colossal east-west fall. Across the gorge a low hill rose like a barrier, a hogback furred by scrubby brush and dwarf trees; what lay beyond it he could not see.

With the sun hot on his cheek he stepped meticulously to the lip of the gorge. The gorge was deep and dark; far below a black stream swirled and eddied, white rills foaming off black boulders. He stepped back and imagined his bridge, gleaming white.

He was streaming sweat and frightened.

He found the bridge of vines, off to the west. The vines were brown-black, three inches thick, wrapped about with tough grasses and layers of leaf, and anchored to a spur of rock. The bridge hung limp against his wall of the gorge. From a gnarled tree on the far lip hung a single vine, down in a slack bow and across to his own side many feet below. The bridge itself, or what he could see of it, looked skimpy, and not a bridge that any man would want to cross every day. He knelt. Far below the water leapt and boiled and beckoned. That was a long way down, and cool and dark. Down there in the spume and the glistening rock. Devils seethed there. If he were a savage he would call it the home of the devils. Unless the cool and the dark were much prized. Heaven might here be cool and moist and dark.

He stood up to dust his knees, and saw a man.

The man stood beside a dense tangle of brush halfway up the hogback across from Morrison. He was lean, and very black, naked and erect. He held a spear, and stared foolishly.

Morrison too stared foolishly.

For many seconds they stood staring. Morrison raised his right hand.

The man raised his spear.

Morrison held forth both hands, empty. The man only stared. Morrison pointed down at the bridge then, and made a lifting motion.

The man stood changeless.

Morrison looked down at the bridge of vines, and beyond to the home of the devils. He felt fear, and stepped back from the lip of the gorge. When he looked up, the man was gone.

4

Some days a wayward wind from the east coasted down off the high land, and a mist of pink dust floated west as the men dug and crushed and tamped. Those days were cooler. The temperature at noon was one hundred and five and not one hundred and ten. Morrison was never bored. The sun was new every morning, and reliable, and not the sun he had known all his life. On his second morning he said to Philips, "I need a hammock." The hot beef and tomatoes were juicy and even the dry biscuit seemed full of flavor. The coffee was thick, bitter mess-hall coffee. All the tastes were like summer and youth, before tobacco and alcohol and sour love.

"We have a couple. The caravan was no good?"

"I got no sleep at all and I almost drowned."

"We will fix you up." He made it sound slangy. In the evening he rigged a hammock close to his own and Ramesh's. "No," he said. "That way you will be stiff in the morning, if you do not fall out. This way. Diagoally." Morrison rocked at peace. Each day the morning light pricked through his roof of leaves and woke him gently, dappling the glade. They walked slowly and talked low. The road inched forward.

Philips had his hands full, his own fault: he was permanently nervous about measurements, contours, coordinates, as if he could not trust numbers, and he uncased his transit at least twice a day, sending Small John or Jacob out with the rod. "Be a sport," Morrison said. "Be a meter off. Nobody will ever know."

"You will know, when you start your bridge."

"Right. Don't be a meter off." That was his own permanent nervousness, and he was uneasy joking about it. After all. It even crossed his mind that the government might fall and a new one order him to cease and desist.

Mornings they all had a plunge before breakfast. Then they repaired to the buffet. Jacob served deftly and Ramesh poured from a huge pot of hot coffee. Small John made a joke. Every morning. The men were various, gloomy or cheery or uncaring, and Morrison was full of the morning: the sun just up, and the river chuckling past, and himself soaking and cool. Crickets and birdsong. There was no mist on the water, but the morning was dank and cool with a green smell, and a coffee smell, and a beef smell; and a man smell and a sun smell. In his youth three smells were summer: sun, hot wood, crushed grass. Here all smells were summer.

He turned brown. Two or three times a week visitors arrived. Their names were Samuel Atlas and Sonny, and they drove two trucks charged with rock. They were stocky, well-bellied, with thick forearms, and they stopped for lunch and went back in other trucks, empty. The men unloaded what they had left.

Tall Boy did the showy work. The others spread rock and then stood back while he rolled it, jouncing and cursing, sweating and singing and shouting like a cowboy in sunglasses and a red fez. Morrison learned names and faces. Tall Boy and Jacob, Big John and Small John and just plain Johnny or Yanni, one called simply Dog, another Villem. Villem was the man with one eye, and close up he looked like a murderer, with a front tooth missing and a complicated scar on one cheek and temple, and a sullen droop to his good eyelid. And Shorty and Frenchy. They had other names on the books, but the books were of no importance or interest. The men said "Good morning boss" and little else. Jacob said nothing, merely nodded. When there was something to be said to or by Morrison, the message came or went by Ramesh.

"I begin to think that you like it here," Philips said after three weeks.

"I do."

"Van Alstyne did not," Philips said with a sly smile, a pimp's grin, grotesque on his strong face. "He liked the women, also beer by the gallon. He was always escaping to the city."

"Not me." Morrison escaped to the gorge. Philips did not know that. Morrison looked for savages.

"There is not much for you to do here. The road is uninteresting."

"The bridge will be interesting. The bridge will be a bitch. How did you get the rope bridge up?"

"The bridge of vines? We never did. We never tried."

"Then how did you map the other approach? From this side? That's not as accurate as I want."

"No," Philips said. "A helicopter came."

Morrison was stunned.

"Is something wrong?"

"No, no. It just hadn't occurred to me."

"We never thought of using the bridge. That is not much of a bridge."

"It took work. They"—whoever they were, and his heart beat stronger—"had to cross the river to the west, there, and come up the mountain. Then somehow they got a line across, and pulled the whole bridge to this side and anchored it. That was a hell of a good breakfast today."

"Tell Ramesh."

"When will the road be finished?"

"Two or three weeks. When does the crane come?"

"Two or three weeks. That's a machine," Morrison said. "By God it is. A most satisfactory machine."

Ramesh had a radio and liked to tell them that France was making trouble "for your country" or that the Vietnamese were rioting, or that China had blown up a hydrogen bomb. They found it hard to care. But when he told Philips that General Ros had marched out of a Cabinet meeting, they cared. Morrison had never heard of General Ros and was not sure what the Cabinet consisted of or what powers it had. But he wanted the government steady and strong. He wanted Goray to be where he was. When the bridge was finished and some ascotted politician had snipped the ribbon, then they could explode, erupt, dismember their fair land; but not before. He was ashamed of that thought but could not deny it. He considered himself with distaste. At least he never said those things aloud. He wondered if all men received vile notions.

He never mentioned the native he had seen. Or that he had dreamed of him one night, he on Morrison's side of the gorge and Morrison on his, frightened, abandoned, night coming on, and Morrison lay flat staring down at the rocks while the native jeered obscenely, and then the walls of the gorge crumbled and Morrison awoke, staring through the leaves at a dead white moon. Saturdays and Sundays, when he was alone, he drove to the gorge and sat waiting, and mimed to an invisible audience. If any. At first it was simple curiosity, the timid fascination of the popeyed tourist; then poetry won out, notions, irrationalities, territorial claims—it was his bridgehead, after all; and then something more, an unease, a necessity, as if what lay on the far side was a destiny. A doom or a glory, a goal. More than just the bridge. As if he were meant to build the bridge only because he was meant to cross this gorge, as if a cave or a cairn or a woman or a wooden chest or a shrine awaited him, marked MORRISON. Or even TO WHOM IT MAY CONCERN; but it was for him. That was more nonsense, like the monkeys and snakes and jungle cats he never saw. But the urgency grew: he must cross on their bridge, and not on his own. When he was there with Philips or the others, he ignored the far side; he wanted something to happen for himself alone.

One night Philips said, "Only sun-worship makes
sense. The sun is the source of all life."

"On this planet," Morrison said. It was after supper
and they were sitting like widows in their little courtyard among the trailers, and gossiping. Ramesh always
lit his lamp and sat on a folding chair. Philips sat on
the doorstep of a trailer, and on moonless nights the
yellow bulb threw shiny planes across his face as he
squinted, pursed his lips, arched his brows. Or hunched
forward, arms on his thighs, head low. From the woods,
night-laughter.

"Other planets are of no interest," Philips said. "I
leave the other planets to the Americans and the Russians, who have solved all their problems on this
one."

The dark was warm and comforting, and the stars
were friendly. There seemed no reason not to enjoy a
third bottle of beer.

"You pig," Philips said. "We are talking theology
and you think only of your pint." The five weeks had
passed like lazy months, and the days and nights of dust
and heat were like so many miles between them and the
world. The world. Meaning anyone anywhere who was
not working on this road and this bridge. So he uncapped a third bottle for Philips too. Ramesh declined.
Ramesh had his pipe. And a small stylet, and every
night he toasted a small pellet and smoked it up. At
first Morrison had no idea what it was. Then he was
shocked. "Let it go," Philips said. But Ramesh came to

him the next day, cheerful and innocent and supple as ever. "I hope you will not mind," he said. "It is only a few grains and I find it pleasant. My health is good, you see. The legends are much exaggerated."

"Well, no, I don't mind," Morrison said, sheepish immediately. None of his business really. Was it. "As long as your health is good. It seems to leave no effects."

"None a-tall," Ramesh said gratefully, and that was that. He smoked it up happily. He belonged to the night as he drowsed, to the land, to the heat. "I am not a slave to it, you see. I could refrain if I wished to. But I do not wish to. Oh no."

Philips smiled faintly hearing that.

Five weeks. Morrison spent Mondays and Tuesdays at the capital with Manoel Serpa and his men. Those were uneasy days. Serpa made him uneasy. The drawings had been rendered with the finest pen-points and the purest ink on the smoothest paper, and the letters and numbers were the pristine work of a master hand, and where Morrison had said one meter twelve he meant one meter twelve and not one meter eleven ninety-nine. Serpa fluttered and placated; absolutely. Absolutely. Absolutely. The forms were perfect, as if cut and joined by Jesus himself. Morrison had only to look. Here. Our Lord was a carpenter. Morrison knew that, did he not. A failed carpenter, Morrison said drily, and Serpa's nose twitched in alarm: a joke? an atheist? He brightened: there. The cement. Of purest white. The best his country could offer. And the little rocks. For the—say that once for me? Ag-gre-gett. And here the retardant, and even so everything covered with wet burlap and sprinkled two-hourly all through the hot night. Feel! Measure!

Serpa was building most of the bridge right there. The killing work, though, would be at the site: they would have to throw one great arch of wooden forms across the gorge and fill it full of concrete and keep the concrete moist while it set. Then Serpa's components, poured, set, and long dry, would be trucked out. And they with their magical crane would swing them out and drop, sidle, edge them into place, slotting and bolting and plating, like tots with a kiddie konstruction kit except that someone, or more, would doubtless die. On a high bridge someone, or more, always did.

And the office claimed him. The office and Isaacson, Utu and Vieira-Souza. And cost sheets (God spare me cost sheets!) and letters from Devoe ("longer reports, please, and considerably more detail. I have not asked before because I know how busy you must be," and so on and so forth). And that bloody hotel. Bloody modern and bloody cool and bloody comfortable. But he could not wait to be out of it. Tuesday evenings he learned that a Land-Rover will do seventy quite nicely, thank you. So skidded into camp with the last light as if fleeing the law; which in a way he was. Ramesh would shout for Jacob then, who served his dinner. He brought back a case of bottled beer, always, on the house, and soon they had built up a good reserve.

Oh he liked those nights. Soft earth and warm air and stars shivering like cold fire. Some nights a monstrous platinum moon, and nothing between you and it.

"Of course, an untouchable," Ramesh said. "Outcaste. Bombay was one great sore, what I remember of it. Oh my God yes. I remember no home. No parent. Only hiding on a dhow, and I did not know where it would go. England perhaps. Well. It went to Aden. If I had been older they would simply have thrown me in. But they laughed, and kept me, and"—he sighed here and nodded, aging suddenly, his rich lips drooping as though memory or wisdom had driven him slack—"and abused me somewhat. After that there was nothing more to learn, so at Aden I ran away and looked for a larger ship. I found one. I have seen all the continents now, except the South Pole."

"Nothing more to learn?"

"Not really."

Morrison was impressed. Imagine having nothing more to learn.

One night he talked too. What do men talk of but themselves? Tossing in a memory, a fact, a small lie. Weaving knots of circumstance to hold lives together: in this place, on this night, there were this Hindu and this Negro and this Irishman, and the Irishman said . . . is that possible? That life is a series of music-hall stories? There were these ten millon Russians and they all got killed. There were these two cities in Japan and then there were not. Once upon a time there was this naked man and woman in a garden. Savages. And if those knots were not tied, was a memory real? If a tree fell and there was no one to hear it fall, would it fall on Morrison? Yes! "A man told me once that I would never know what was real because I was white and had never starved. But I bet neither of you has ever been horsewhipped. I have." Philips and Ramesh stirred at this reversal, this disorder of nature. "In nineteen-forty," Morrison said. "I got caught with a girl, in a barn, and her father whipped us. Both of us. Not a horsewhip really. Just a little buggy whip. But it hurt like hell. Finally"—and once more he swallowed down the bitter memory—"I just ran," swallowed it down for the thousandth time, the same ache, the same shame, the same dumb, blind rage at himself, at her, at the old man, at a universe that rewarded love with lashes. "Small towns," he said. "Everybody knew about it. My father thought it was very funny. He was a house-painter who got drunk every Saturday night. Peaceful man. My mother didn't think it was so funny. She died the next year. Just got tired of things and died. By then I was gone. Not exactly whipped out of town, but I didn't seem to have much to say to anybody."

"Foolish people," Philips said. "Whipping children for that."

"Yes. I wonder sometimes if the whip made scars on her," with rage and shame again like rot in his mouth. "I tried to cover her up, and I remember her breasts shivering. It was in the afternoon. Then I just ran."

"You should not dwell on it," Philips said.

"No. With a fine war in between, and so forth, you'd think I'd have forgotten by now. But I wake up sometimes," he burst out, "and the shame is awful. Not that I got caught with a girl and not that I was whipped;

but that I ran and left her. I never saw her again. My God," he groaned, "we never even *finished*."

"That was more than a quarter of a century ago," Ramesh said. "We all hurt people. We all hate to remember hurting. But if you are clever enough to be an engineer, you are clever enough to survive such a silly thing."

"Oh no," Morrison said. "I'm not clever. I'm not really smart at all. Except with numbers, maybe, shapes, spaces. I'm slow. I like being slow but I don't know enough. About myself even." Many brilliant men skittered across the surface of his century and he could not say that he understood them, their intensity, their nervousness, the stuttering light they shed. Nor could he say that he had tried very hard to understand them. When he wrestled ponderously with a new idea, he was always disappointed to find that it was an old idea. Or nonsense. Brilliant men seemed proud and defensive and so could not be trusted. "I'm not even making sense, I suppose." He had built a highway in the northern autumn, riding a grader sleepily and happily among elms and maples, brown in the V of his shirt, and it was a time of great crisis, or so said the newspapers, and he rode his grader aware that the earth might gape to engulf him but taking it on faith that a road was worth building. "Faith. I don't know what that is. Everybody has to die but nobody has to break his word." He stopped short. After an embarrassed and burbling swig he went on: "Don't laugh at me. I was a faithful husband. Twice."

"Now you are bragging." Philips smiled. "But I

know what you are getting at, I think. You are wondering how long until the next catastrophe."

"Yes. Yes. You remember King Midas? I feel like a new kind of Midas, a twentieth-century Midas: except when I'm working, everything I touch turns to carrion. Senecas and redwoods and wives."

"What are Senecas?" Ramesh asked.

"Senecas are people who believe promises."

"And what are wives?" Philips asked.

Morrison was silent.

"They were unfaithful?"

"Both of them," he cried in sudden outrage. "Nobody cares any more. Even about that. They were upset that I minded."

"Here we do not worry so much about that," Philips said. "Maybe you were not so good with women."

"I guess not," Morrison mumbled, knowing that for the truth. "Both times it lasted two years." His heart quailed then and he went on: "All right: the second one was only a repeat. Desperation. My fault. But I loved my first wife. The way," he stumbled, "the way they tell you you ought to love truth and justice and things like that."

"Truth and justice are not things," Philips said. "What happened?"

"I wish I knew. It was wild for about a year and then —oh, hell!" He wrenched the words out: "There was somebody else all the time. And we kept on trying for another year and finally I hated her." He sat back empty. "She was all flesh. Nothing but flesh." And I am grow-

ing old and not worth much these days. Not for a year
now. He heard the words but knew that he had not said
them aloud.

"So are you," Philips said. "What is wrong with
that?"

"The flesh is nothing," Ramesh said.

"The flesh is everything," Philips said. "You should
have beaten her." He was half joking.

"That is the advantage of arranged marriages," Ramesh said sweetly. "The man has not agreed to be agreeable. He has only agreed to be married."

"We tried," Morrison said. "She was very beautiful.
Not too bright. She wore sunglasses with rhinestones in
the frames. By the end of the second year she was only
lumpy flesh. Mornings were horrible. I suppose I'm not
altogether normal about this." If you only knew!

"Well, I am," Philips said grimly. "Along about
Thursday I become very lonesome."

And Ramesh said, "None of it matters. We live for a
tick of the watch only."

"No preaching," Philips said. "I have no wish to be
reborn a locust."

"You will be reborn a baboon," Ramesh said, "spill-
ing yourself every three minutes with a different fe-
male."

Philips said dolefully, "If only I could be sure of that."

Morrison grieved. Could they see his face? "The most
flesh I ever saw was in the war. I told you I was an orderly, a medic. We were using the downstairs of a farmhouse, and after a while there was only the doctor and

me and the wounded. We never knew what happened
to everybody else, but later we found dead men outside.
It was as if the whole war had swept by and not touched
us but left us all this work to do. All of them lying there
moaning and yelling. We shot them full of morphine
and hauled them up on a big table and the doctor did
what he could. We were already a long time without
sleep and I think we lasted forty-eight hours or so." He
groaned. Ramesh nodded sadly. "Arms and legs. Heads
torn open. Eyes hanging down. There was one man—"
He shuddered. "He was hit in the belly. When we cut his
pants away there was nothing between his legs. Only
blood. And he was still breathing. Christ!"

"What did you do?" Philips's voice was surly.

"Killed him. Put him down and let him die. Pretty
soon the doctor passed out, just fell forward into somebody's insides and then slid down to the floor. So I went
out looking for people and found them and told them,
and then I collapsed. They sent me back to Paris and
then home. I told them I would rather spend my life
in jail than go back. So they decided I was a psycho and
let me out."

"Good," Philips said. "You were lucky."

"I saw a man beheaded once," Ramesh said. "In
China. Before the war. With a sword. Oh, that was
something. Damn and blahst, that was something."

"I never saw anything like that," Morrison said.
"Except for the war. My life was very dull for a long
time."

"When did you see your first corpse?" Philips asked.

"In the war."

"Very late. You were not prepared."

"No," Morrison said. "I grew up in a little town where nothing happened."

"Only horsewhipping," Philips said.

"Where was that?" asked Ramesh the world-traveler.

"Upstate New York."

"Ah, New York," Ramesh said.

"No," Morrison said. "You're thinking of the city. Everybody thinks of the city. But there's a whole state too, full of cattle and apple trees and small towns with Dutch names."

"Dutch names!" Ramesh was delighted. "Like here."

"The names are sometimes like here," Morrison said, "but not the rest of it." He smiled, feeling lighter, rested. "I'm making myself homesick. Let's talk about something else."

A hairy spider trundled into their courtyard and stood, indecisive, four inches long, thick of body. Philips stalked it cautiously and hammered it flat with a sandal. "Excuse me," he said politely to Ramesh. "I hope it was not a loved one."

Ramesh was peeved.

Morrison and Philips stood beneath a white sky with their backs to the gorge. The men sat or sprawled but were attentive. Philips told them why they were there, speaking in that bubbly bastard language, and then subsided and gestured at Morrison. "Soon we start on the bridge," Morrison said, and Philips translated.

Morrison told them how the bridge would be built. They were a good audience, motionless, his and Philips's absolutely. He spoke for no more than five minutes because he knew that what he said was not important. It was important only that they hear something directly from the boss.

"Then there will be six or eight wire men. Before we pour the concrete we will set hundreds of steel rods in place. These add great strength to the concrete. Then there will be the concrete men and finishers. The concrete must be carefully mixed and after it is poured it must be kept moist until it sets. How many here have worked with concrete before?"

Hands rose: a dozen.

"Then you know what I am talking about. Please explain all that you know to the others. And I want you all to see these drawings. Let every man see them to be sure he understands the work. Talk about them. Each crew will have its own foreman, who will do more explaining as we move into the work.

"One thing." He spoke sharply and they watched him closely. "The various pieces of the bridge will fit together perfectly. In some places there will be slots and tongues to fit into the slots. In other places there will be holes drilled for bolts. Or flat depressions for steel plates. The fitting must be exact. Everything must be exact. If anything is set carelessly the whole bridge will be spoiled. Any man who works carelessly will be sent away. Philips will tell you more. So will Ramesh. Orders must be obeyed exactly. And every man must be careful not to fall, not to bump others, not to hit men or materials with moving objects. Keep your eyes open and your hands sure. We will work carefully even if it means working slowly."

Dog spoke: how would they reach the far side for blasting, and to start that end of the arch?

"There is a bridge of vines," Morrison said.

Philips was startled. The men muttered.

Morrison laughed and shook his head. "Take it easy. The crane will swing us across. On a platform."

The muttering ceased but there were no smiles. Philips spoke again. "I told them you were making a joke," he said. "They do not care for joking about the bridge."

"They're right," Morrison said. "Go over it again. Stress caution. Tell them I'm through making jokes."

While Philips lectured, Morrison inspected the far side. The dazzle brought tears to his eyes; he squinted. Hillside, brush, trees. No motion; only the sunlight and the drowsy slope. And the gorge between, and bird-call far below. The gorge looked very cool. And to the west that long lovely roll of green. Philips bubbled on, then called: "They want to know who will do the blasting."

"You and I," he called back. "Tell them about the drills and how they work. Tell them the diamonds are of no value so not to steal them."

Many times now he had stood here alone and looked for a sign. His wasted weekends. Eminent explorer seeks Saturday spoor. But he wondered who these people were and what they would think of his bridge. Also it would not do to suffer showers of arrows at critical

moments. Somewhere in there was the border; a few
miles from him was the Portagee side. Probably no
man had ever crossed over from here. He thought of
the Portagee side as an abrupt alteration in terrain;
perhaps a river, or a sudden strip of yellow grass. Maybe
a double white line; he grinned. A shame to come so
far and not see it. And those people. Perhaps there were
no people. Perhaps he had seen a roving hunter.

Philips had fallen silent. He gestured languidly and
the men drifted back to the fringe of trees.

A roving hunter. The thought saddened Morrison.
Where the hell am I going? What am I? A speech-
maker. He was very angry for no reason. Imparting
wisdom to ditch-diggers in a far place. Looking for
primitives like a tourist. Nothing left of me. Good only
for this, exile and playing with blocks. South Pole next.
Take Ramesh, who has never been there.

Then he was ashamed. What the hell. You must be
lonesome.

It occurred to him that it would be cheering to have
a friend. Or to enjoy a woman.

Or at least to get a cold drink inside him.

"I do not understand you," Philips said amiably. "You
must have a girl that you see on Monday nights."

"No. I just haven't felt like weekends. Next week,
maybe." It was Saturday at noon and the men were
gone, the trucks had coughed and roared off, and Philips and Ramesh were making ready.

"But five weeks," Philips said. "That is a long time

with no play. Positively abnormal."

˙   Ramesh was packing a small bag. Pursed lips, fussy darting hands. Socks. What for?

"I'll go in with you next week."

"Good. You are spoiling us."

One of the three remained always at the camp. Morrison had stood guard with pleasure.

"Ah. Toussex," Ramesh said.

"You don't really take all those."

"I like to have them with me," Ramesh said. "One never knows. Germs. A cough."

Morrison examined the kit. "Toussex. That's for coughs. Ephedros. That must be a cold in the nose. Veganine. Headache. Hepanil. What's that?"

"For disturbances of the liver," Ramesh said. "Would you like to read the accompanying literature?"

"No thank you."

"You must always read the accompanying literature. There are reactions to beware of."

"I thought Indians weren't suppose to kill things. Even germs."

"But I intend to live to be one hundred," Ramesh said. He snapped shut the kit.

"Ah. You don't want to escape the cycle. I thought nothingness was the great goal."

"There is plenty of time for nothingness," Ramesh said. "There is all eternity. We live for only a tick of the watch."

"A hundred years."

"A tick of the watch."

"Come on," Philips said, in the Land-Rover.

Ramesh sat primly beside him, hands folded.

"Next week," Philips said. "I want to see you in action."

"Next week," Morrison said, and blessed them as they sped away.

5

Mother Martha's place stood on a hillside and faced
west, so the sun was behind them and low when Philips
bucked the Land-Rover up a rutted track, raced it
through a stand of palms with the horn wailing, and
jammed it to a halt under the eaves. Approximately
eaves. Mother Martha's was mainly an open shed, a roof
some seventy-five feet long on posts. The roof, or what
Morrison could see of it, was tin here and thatch there,
and they were parked under a tangled overhang of
thatch. There were wooden tables and stools and
benches scattered outside. Men were drinking with girls
in bright blouses, and they shouted at Tall Boy and Philips, who shouted too and waved.

Inside, in the dim light, the chatter was low; on the
tables were oil lamps, unlit. Cases of bottled beer stood
in stacks. Masks hung from the dark beams; also animal skulls with antlers or tusks. The bartender was
ebony-bald with jolly wide eyes and a grinning wide
mouth. Philips said, "Emanuel. Morrison," and they
shook hands. "Three beers," Philips said. He slapped

his wallet to the bar. "Give me your money."

Morrison obeyed. Philips counted the bills and joined them to his own. When the bottles were uncapped, he thrust the wallet at Emanuel. "Give it to Martha. Right now."

"Okay." Emanuel beamed.

"Cheers," Philips said, and drank off half a bottle. "The money is not needed and would only make trouble. Emanuel keeps track. If you have a girl, she tells Martha."

"Credit. Even that. Is there a discount for volume?"

"No need to be coarse," Philips said, and wiped his mouth. "There is more to it than just 'that.' Believe me. I wish we could take a couple back."

"You never talk about women at the camp."

"What would I say? They are there, or they are not there."

Behind the bar stood battalions of bottles: only rum and whisky, and something called Martini. No soda, no ginger ale, no quinine water. No glasses either. Morrison sighed.

"What?"

"The drinking will be serious. Is there food at least?"

"Oh yes. Back there is Martha's little flat and a kitchen. Meat, tomatoes, and fruit. Beef, goat, pork. But the stress is on drinking." He grinned, and finished his beer. "Also cigarettes and straw fans. Aspirin and bandages. And that sums it up. Also several shacks out back." He grinned again. "And several thousand square miles of soft earth and waving grasses."

"Restful."

"Wrong."

Night fell and the lamps were lit. Moths emerged, suicides; flames plucked at them; they shriveled in silence. The shed filled, and noise rose, laughter, arguments, the static of a careless crowd. The three men had progressed to rum. Morrison was hungry, but what was the etiquette? Tall Boy was already dreamy and had begun to hum and mutter. Philips was running on about the government, apparently the most agreeable and flexible faction of bandits available and therefore to be supported. Morrison was jittery. Many glanced at him and quickly away, and once a newcomer blinked and looked again, as if Morrison were a polar bear. The girls too glanced, more openly, and it was Morrison who looked away. With a ripple of bitterness. He might try. But failure here would not be private; there was a whole country to laugh. So he looked away.

The shed roared and clattered. Morrison was gloomy and hungry. Women squeezed by, and a light hand brushed his neck; a giggle. He realized that he was exotic, and cheered up, but only a bit. Somewhere someone sang. The rum was doing nothing for him. He missed the road.

"Smile," Philips said. "Saturday night. Big time. A moment snatched from death and eternity."

"You missed your calling," Morrison said.

Mirth: white teeth. "Philips in Paris," Philips said.
"Beret. Cigarette-holder. Petals on a wet black bough."

"Petals?"

"Poetry, man."

"Oh. I know some poetry," Morrison said. "Birth
death and fornication. Not with a bang but a whimper.
A bunch of the boys were whooping it up in the Malemute Saloon."

"Malemute?"

"Poetry, man."

"Oh. You know William Faulkner?"

"I know who he was."

Philips despaired. "Do you read nothing at all?"

"Magazines. Newspapers."

"Junk and lies," Philips said.

"Garbage," Morrison agreed. "Shakespeare, when I
was a boy."

"But after all he is not for grown men."

"Oh, shut up. I'm an engineer."

"What need the bridge much broader than the
flood?"

"What?"

"The first rule, you see. Economy. That is Shake-
peare."

"No kidding." He was cheered again. "That's pretty
good."

A man leaned between them to stare at him. He had
a hand on Philips's shoulder. A light shade he was, coffee with milk, and a breath on him like blue meat. "Philips," he chimed. "How you going?"

"All right. You?"

"Good enough."

"This is Snyder," Philips said. "This is Morrison my boss. Synder is with the immigration. Wears a white uniform."

"Pleased to know you," Snyder said. "No uniform Saturday night." He skirted the table and took Tall Boy's stool. Tall Boy was gone, somewhere. "How you like this country?" Morrison could barely hear him; the shed was alive with sound, smoke, motion.

"I like it fine."

"Good. Very good. Have a pleasant stay." To Philips he said, "That Craddock here."

"I saw him come in. You mean he wants more?"

"No, nobody ever know what he wants. Just came to tell you."

"No trouble," Philips said. "But thank you."

"Good. I leave you now. Pleased to know you," and he shook hands with Morrison, leaning across the table, nodding, earnest. Then he was gone.

"What was that?"

"Oh, I had some trouble," Philips said. "Some time ago. The usual beery discussion, followed by athletics."

"How did you do?" Morrison could not remember when he had last struck a blow.

"Won handily. I would say about two minutes of the third round."

"Congratulations. I don't much care for it myself."

"I know. No one will bother you here."

Morrison looked the question.

"No. Just elementary courtesy to a guest of the republic."

"Good."

"No one cares that much, you know. You are a curiosity and nothing more. I wonder at it sometimes. How quickly we forget grudges. We here, I mean."

"We do too," Morrison said. "Everybody loves Germany now."

"And Japan?"

"I don't remember ever hating them."

"Good." Philips drank deeply from the bottle, and then from a bottle of water, and pushed them at Morrison. "Live, man."

"You bet, man."

"Oh come on," Philips said. "Enjoy yourself a bit. Maybe you want a girl."

"Not now. Where's Tall Boy?"

"Out in the bushes, I expect."

Morrison grunted. "What do I do for a bathroom?"

"A bathroom?"

"A privy."

"Outside, but downhill. Uphill is love, downhill is reality."

"Reality is always downhill."

"A philosopher," Philips groaned. "Just watch where you put your feet."

"We must do something about this man," Philips said to Tall Boy. A peal, a squeal of laughter, commotion in a corner; nothing.

"I'll be all right," Morrison said.

"I am not so sure. What about it, Tallie? Can you recommend a companion for Hamlet here? Someone spiritual."

Tall Boy grinned uneasily and drank from the bottle.

"I worry about you," Philips went on.

"Don't. Just leave me alone."

"You reject modern plumbing and countless servants. You abjure the luxurious life of an American in foreign parts. You drink with the boys. But not with the girls."

"Forget it," Morrison said.

"No, no." His eyes had reddened. His voice cut through the noise, and yet it was soft. "We must have someone here who would please you."

"I'm not in the mood." Morrison took up the bottle.

"Not in the mood. Well. You know," Philips said, "while we have only the one color, we have many shades. Am I right, Tallie?"

"Right," Tall Boy boomed.

"Shut your mouth," Morrison said to Philips, and cursed him aloud.

Tall Boy's eyes were wide.

"You hold on now," Philips said low. "Just hold on."

Morrison cursed him again. "You come with me."

Philips cocked his head in curiosity. "A scrimmage?" he said, with some pleasure. Then he stood up and Morrison marched him to the bar. The drinkers looked at him and made room. He was close enough to see the red veinlets in Philips's wary eyes. "You smart son of a bitch," Morrison said. "And in front of Tall Boy. You can have my job when I go home. Not before."

Philips said, "I do not want your job."

"Then get off my back. And shut up about women."

"Your lack of interest is impolite. And intriguing."
He must have thought he was being elegantly insolent.
Morrison was suddenly sorry for him, and saw African
potentates in silk hats. Curling lips.

"Horseshit," he said. "Now you listen to me. What
problems I have with women are none of your god-damn
business. Understand? They are also not local and have
nothing to do with color or shade. Understand? At
the moment I am not a healthy buck like you. Got it?"

"Never call me a buck," Philips said tightly.

"Then don't call me a white fag."

After a moment Philips looked away. Then he said,
easier, "Problems."

"Problems. Mine. None of your business."

After a longer silence Philips nodded. "Okay. Let's go
drink."

At the table he went on: "Tallie, I was rude to the
boss. Forget this whole thing."

Tall Boy grinned again. "Yay, I got other things to
remember. That Lollie in the red shirt."

"I remember Lollie," Philips said. "By God I remember Lollie. Very important to remember Lollie."

"Very important," Tall Boy approved.

"The greatest importance. The only importance."

"Do you really think that?" Morrison's anger was
gone.

"*Their* only importance," Philips said.

"Talk about impolite," Morrison said. "The bottle, please. That's the lowest opinion of women I ever heard."

Philips slid the bottle forward and shrugged. "Different in your country, maybe. A great mistake, I would say. Tallie, get us another bottle, will you? Look at everything important that happens. That has ever happened. Men did it. The world is moved by men. In a man's world women never do anything important for the sake of the work. They do it to prove they can do it."

"Joan of Arc."

"An hysteric. A virgin," with lofty scorn.

"Madame Curie."

"You see," Philips said. "There are so few exceptions that you can name them."

"Queen Elizabeth. The first."

"One woman," Philips said, "who had a hundred good men around her. *They* did the work. The thinking. The fighting. But I will give you her. I will even give you Christina. She made a mess of things but she was strong. Not strong enough, though, and her weaknesses were a woman's. When things were hardest she passed as a man."

"Who was she?"

"What do you learn in American schools? Queen of Sweden. Seventeenth century."

"Greta Garbo."

Philips laughed. They were feeling much better. "Yes. God help you. Greta Garbo."

Tall Boy sat down. With two bottles. "Save a trip,"

he said. Save ah treep. The rum was suddenly delicious. Morrison rolled it on his tongue and gargled discreetly. Saturday night. Tall Boy's scarlet fez. All these people having a fine time. From the Jomo Kenyatta Room of Mother Martha's Mahatma Motel, on the road to— where? what? Happy screams, happy shouts. Outside a radio, music, a man and a woman dancing, circling, backing, bumping, grinding. Teeth and sweat. Her blouse came off. Hips rolling. Breasts hanging, atremble. Arms high: whirl: atremble. Stomp, glide, shimmy. Soft and black like the night.

At some point hot goat's meat and cold tomatoes, and a grotesque grapefruit called an ugly. Always the rum. Man, you are killing yourself. Philips found another pitcher of water. The meat was stringy and sharp. More dancers. At the bar, singing, mournful, a heavy beat. Always the friendly rum. "Philips. How you goin?" Woman-smell. The air hot, eddies of smoke. A dog lifting a leg at the stacked beer. "Tall Boy. How you?" Lamplight flickered, shadows swooped. "We came out in a Dakota," Philips was saying. "A live sheep, in a crate, a thousand pounds of local tobacco, and several cases of rum. Twenty-two of us and one Englishman, a chemist and teacher. A bucket-chemist, he called himself. Long and blond and with one of those high whiny Manchester street-boy voices. And you know the runnels down the floor of a Dakota? Well, the sheep pissed. And it ran down the runnel and past the Englishman, slow and dark yellow, and he came awake and looked

at the cases of rum and smiled. Then he bent down and
dipped a long professorial finger into it. No one moved
or said a word. And then with that faraway look, deep
concentration, expertise, the little wrinkles between the
eyes, he licked his finger. Slowly, judiciously. Then he
nodded, the sure, serious nod of the connoisseur, and fell
asleep again. No one said a word then or later. But
when we were off the plane and got into the trucks at
the airstrip, and he was by the door of his private car,
he turned to wave good-bye, and I led the men in three
cheers. Hip-hip. You never saw a man so pleased. Right
now at his club in London he is telling somebody about
the natural and spontaneous love of blacks for the English."

God, the energy. Song and dance and merry story,
lurch and lunge, shout and spin in the smoky shed, and
the moths flitting to death. Animal masks glowed blue-
black; faces too, wet mouths. "Where's Tall Boy now?"

"Where indeed," Philips said, pleased. "Spreading
cheer. A busy bee. How doth the busy bee improve each
shining houri."

"What?"

"Good God. A bachelor of science."

"Master. Magister." not French

"But what do you know? You must know something
besides numbers."

"A little French," Morrison said promptly, "and music. I know good music. The blessings of radio. Always

while I work, in the office. Scarlatti is best for engineers."

"There," Philips said, much relieved. "Give thanks.
A noble art. The Albert Hall. Bach Beethoven Brahms."

"Fela Sowande."

Philips foundered. "But he is Nigerian. How do you
know about him?"

"Oh well," Morrison said, and smiled airily.

"French, music, and drawing," Philips murmured.
"You sound like a most Victorian young lady." But he
meant no harm.

A lull. An ebb, and a gathering. The voices low, the
radio noticeably loud. The second bottle was almost
gone; it must have been late. But they had the third.
They were speaking of women when Tall Boy padded in
and sat down happily. "What I don't see," Morrison was
complaining unsteadily, "is how any European seduced a
woman before nineteen-twenty. Byron. Liszt. All those
Casanovas. It must have taken days to get all the clothes
off them. Time for husbands to come home, children to
wake up, whole cities to burn down."

"What is he saying?" Tall Boy wanted to know.

"He is an historian," Philips said.

"What is that?"

"Drink your rum."

"Where did you get that hat?" Morrison asked, and
Tall Boy removed it gravely and set it on Morrison's
head. Where it settled to the brows.

"Stylish," Philips said. "Suits you. Makes a new man of you."

"Inch'allah," Morrison said.

Some time later Philips was missing, and Tall Boy was missing, and Morrison was alone, far from home, in boozy repose. He was wondering if Philips and he would become friends. Then he forgot Philips and peered around him at the boiling crowd. There was no going home on Saturday night. A thought: Christianity's gift to the heathen was not Sunday morning but Saturday night. He tried to see himself then as they saw him, and was disturbed. He knew too many engineers who worked abroad and went home rarely or never; had no home, really, but the job. Had plenty of dusky servants and no manners. No wives, most of them. Thick men usually because they worked hard and were well fed. They drank too much because that was their mask; they lived up to drawings in adventure magazines. Hung together and fought each other in brawls sparked by false manhood. "You got to have balls in this business," they would say. And count their native women for each other. And then retire to Panama or Florida or the Philippines, with more dusky servants, and live happily ever after swimming in gin and cursing inferior breeds and the second Roosevelt. And Morrison was one of them, maybe. Bwana Sahib Tuan. "Nobody in this world was ever *exactly* six feet tall," one of them had threatened him. "You know why? Because Jesus Christ was exactly six feet tall, that's why. And he was perfect." Baked-brick face.

From that slough of despond he turned his thoughts to the bridge. The overhang of the roadway would cast a graceful shadow on the arching wall beneath. With the sun high the road would gleam and the arch would be cool and floating, all shadowed. With the sun low the bridge would shine white at a distance. He saw it in those lights; in moonlight; under cloud. Mysterious in star-light hanging pale above nothing. Truly floating then. One straight white line, and a white arch beneath. Pure.

Closer up it would be very different. The men who built it would know what tangles of steel slept within the concrete, and what streams of crushed stone; what mastic cushioned sections, what chemistry bound the whole. In a hundred degrees of heat a man who could not write his name would talk knowingly of retarding densifiers, and would tell you ever after, in teachers' tones, that without them concrete will set too quickly in great heat, and will be weak. And I had a lucky stone, he would say, a green lucky stone that I always carried, and I threw it in when we poured the center section. Yes sir. My *luck* is in that bridge.

Morrison's luck seemed to be in the bottle before him. Even the bridge bored him. Saturday night.

What about a woman? What do you care what people think? And maybe it would be good, perfect, early times with Joanne.

Joanne. Silly piece. And what did you want more than a silly piece? Brains of solid gold, but you knew that all

along. Curlers. God strike dead all women in curlers,
now and forever, and blight their improbable descend-
ants.

Joanne! My fault. I wanted a silly piece and that is exactly what I got. My fault. And that woman today, gentlemen, is . . . where? Gone. Years. Married, doubtless. Six kids. Curlers in the supermarket. Those sunglasses.

And that man today, ladies, is a surly eunuch boozing
it up on a hill in the jungle and weeping rummy tears
for himself.

So he stood up, blinking, lacking youth and vigor,
joyless, and took the bottle by the neck and wandered
uphill. Reality is downhill, love is uphill.

He heard first the silence and then the shouts, and quit
dawdling.

He had not known what to expect: a primitive rite,
an orgy, perhaps lady wrestlers. What he found was the
classic circle of safely exuberant bystanders, in the glow
of the shed, ringing a brawl. Delight, bloodlust,
screeched advice. Swelling murmurs. Laughter. He
moved unnoticed this once, seeking Philips, taking
pleasure in the warm press of dark bodies, the comfortable crush of a whistling, hooting, nickering crowd.
Girls straddled their men's napes, skirts rucked high,
long black thighs gleaming, heels hugging hard flanks.

He found Philips. Kid Philips. In this corner. Main at-
traction. A moment later Philips was on the ground, and

a moment after that, as if the roar had borne him up, he was on his feet. The other fellow, Craddock probably, was taller and slower. As Philips danced and grinned, queasiness twisted Morrison. A chill. A large man beside him shouted, "Hit him, Craddock! Hit him, Craddock!" Morrison was turning to retreat when Philips hit Craddock full on the temple, and Craddock fell to one knee, and the man beside Morrison raged shrilly and lumbered forward.

Well, Morrison was not much for fraternity and such, no, but in any crew there is a loose solidarity, the tighter when you, or they, may be killed on the job. All big bridges took lives, and many small ones. Heights. Swinging booms. Defective materials and a grafter banking. So he was cold and afraid, and wanted to be anywhere else, but stepped out all the same, and took the man by the shoulder and said, "Where you going?"

Without an audience the man might have subsided, and God knows Morrison would have. But Morrison was a visitor of note, it seemed, and the crowd hushed, and his man snarled. Then Craddock was up, and Philips moved in swiftly, and Morrison's man shook himself loose and drew back a ponderous left fist. He seemed to be making lengthy preparations for a roundhouse blow; to be recalling instructions, and consulting ethereally with a possible manager. Perhaps it was the illusion of slow motion, of stasis even, often evoked by critical moments. Morrison had infinite time and was infinitely aware; time to swallow once, to set his back teeth together, to sense his own cold fear and the hot excitement of a hundred strangers. Time to know that whatever he did, he was wrong. Time to think that he might be hurt, and to feel foolish at the thought; time to remember that he was a coward, but to remember too that pain passed like cold or thirst.

So Morrison walloped the man with a good hard right hand, and felt it all the way up his arm, in his chest, his throat, his eyes. Not the impact, not the shock. Far worse: the satisfaction. Like love: his heart swelled. The man dropped and sprawled, and Morrison felt huge. The man gathered himself and sat up, blinking, pressing his jaw with both hands; and pouting then, like an unwarned child spanked unjustly; pouting without rancor.

Blessed are the peacemakers. The crowd was silent. Philips and Craddock stood watching. To Philips Morrison gestured his helplessness, palms up, shrugging. Philips spoke to Craddock in the local language, and then to the crowd. Someone laughed, and called out a joke; others laughed. Even Morrison's victim smiled. Craddock left the circle, which broke up; Morrison's man, with a last musing glance, shanked off; Philips joined Morrison and they stood quietly.

"Hurt your hand?"

"A little. Was that Craddock?"

"Yes."

"Who did I hit?"

"Fellow named Cook," Philips said. "A cab driver."

"Well." Morrison was stupidly content. "Time for a drink. Do I have to keep looking over my shoulder?"

"No. It is finished for tonight. If he comes to the

table, offer him the bottle and drink after him. Why did you hit him?"

"I hate cab drivers," Morrison said. By heaven he felt good. He felt so good he wanted to cry.

He unfurled a kerchief to wipe his brow, and found that he was still wearing Tall Boy's fez.

The sun woke him, late. Emanuel had strung a hammock for him between two leafy trees. The sun glared from the hilltop, brightening his bower. A yawn and a stretch. His watch told him the hour was ten. All about him, silence, golden sunlight, broad leaves limp. He sat up in the hammock and rocked playfully. Clear head, muddy mouth. Hunger. Through the brush he saw the shed; no one. He made his way inside. Still no one. Behind the bar he found a spigot, and twisted, and water gushed, cold. He felt for the fez: gone. Reclaimed. When? No matter. He bowed his head beneath the spigot. The water was cold on his neck and chest. He drank freely, spat, drank again. Then he stood in the sunlight to dry, and then he sat lizardlike at a table and dreamed of food.

After many minutes he heard footsteps, and turned. A woman came to lean against a post. She was in her fifties, perhaps, medium of figure and plain of face, wearing a print dress, yellow cloth and red flowers. "Good morning," he said.

"Good morning." Her face was pleasant, her eye quick. Her hair was frizzy and short. He saw that her legs were quite bowed, and she was barefoot. "Look," she said suddenly, and pointed beyond him.

It was a yellow parrot with a blue-green beak, high in a tree near Morrison's hammock.

"Pretty," he said. "When I came here I looked for animals like a little boy. Jungle cats, monkeys. But I haven't seen much." He rose. "My name is Morrison."

"I know," she said. "I am Martha."

"How do you do."

She nodded.

"Sit down?"

"No. Not yet. You probably want to eat."

"Yes. Anything."

"You sit down. I will get you fruit and coffee."

"Thank you. Will you have some with me?"

She smiled faintly. "All right. Just coffee."

She was a plain woman but graceful, and seemed amused by him. Why not? A queer guest he was. The word came to him: chatelaine. Being a chatelaine is sometimes in the set of the shoulders and the quick but calm eye.

A spider scuttled across his table and down. The parrot spoke: one hoarse caw. The sun was hotter now and he moved inside, under the roof, and took another table. The boulevardier and the chatelaine. Des fruits et deux filtres.

"Quite a time last night," she said. She bore papayas and uglies in a basket; on the tray, coffee things.

"Oh yes," he said. "Do you mind if I begin? I'm dying. I hope I didn't disgrace myself." Sweet papaya! Juicy papaya!

She poured coffee. "Sugar?"

"Two, thank you. And milk."

"Goat's milk."

"Fine. I didn't see you last night."

"Not Saturdays. I like it quiet."

"Do you really keep all the bills in your head?"

"No." That made her laugh. "For a few only. Philips is one. I am glad he is not my son—he is wild—but he is an honest man. He lacks kindness. He is so honest that he hurts people."

"Why is that? Do you know?"

"No. Maybe that preacher who gave him a home. Some people steal like breathing. He is honest like breathing."

Morrison nodded, accepting that, and sliced more papaya. "None for you? Sure?"

"Sure. I ate. Why did you hit Cook?"

He told her.

"That is all right then," she said cheerfully. "He is not a bad man. You should know that."

"It had nothing to do with good or bad."

"You were wearing a Muslim hat. Are you a Muslim?" She sipped elegantly at her black coffee; her little finger crooked.

"No. That was Tall Boy's hat."

"Christian?"

"Yes and no." It was the local way and he did not mind. A foreigner was fair game and could be asked all questions. "My father was Catholic and my mother Baptist, and neither of them cared too much. So I am nothing. If you mean do I believe in heaven and hell, the answer is no. And if you don't believe in that, there's not much reason to believe the rest." It came to him then: "This is Sunday morning. Is that why you ask? Are you a Christian?"

"I am like you," she said. "When I need religion I talk to the sky."

"I'm much worse than that," he said. "When I need religion I talk to myself. Are there many Christians here?" Small talk in the bois on Sunday morning.

"Oh yes. Many Christians and many Hindus, and still many who talk to the trees and the rain. And many who have nothing. Some of your people are here. They have a radio station, and they sell radios cheap, and talk about Jesus. Every day of the week. They tell about young people who die of cancer but are happy because of Jesus."

"Oh."

"You had no woman," she said.

"I don't want to talk about it."

"All right," she said. "Why do you come here and not go to town? The big hotel."

"I go there when I have work in town," he said. "Otherwise I like to be near the job. I came here with Philips. He said it was a good place."

"For a wild one like him it is."

"Well, I like it too." He smiled. "Any more coffee?"

"Here. Is it?"

"Is it what?"

"A good place?"

"Oh yes." He smiled again. "Things happen. The last

time I hit a man must have been twenty years ago. And
he hit me back."

A gust of laughter shook her; she threw off hoots
and cackles like a fruit tree in a gale, and the morning
was littered with her pleasure.

"I want to be delivered from the flesh," Tall Boy said,
while Philips rolled his eyes in mockery. "Yes. I am a
Baptist man."

"On Sunday morning you are a Baptist man," Philips
said. "The rest of the week you are a liar, a thief, a brag-
gart, a drunkard, and a fornicator."

"Leave him be," Martha said. "He is just back from
church and let him feel pure for an hour."

"He is also out of his head and sleepy," Philips said.
"He never slept last night. He went straight from rut to
Jesus."

Tall Boy bowed his head and suffered. They were all
eating cold meat and drinking beer, some time after
noon.

"You have a rough mouth," Martha said. "Leave him
be."

"Right," Morrison said. "A little God won't hurt
him."

Philips scoffed. "Hark hark the clerk. I thought you
were a heathen like the rest of us."

"I am. He isn't. Respect it."

Tall Boy blessed him with warm eyes and stared
sternly at Philips. It was suddenly obvious that he loved
Philips. Morrison's eyes met Martha's.

"Respect it!" Philips scorned him again. "I respect Tallie. Not his fairy tales."

"Then forget about them. They don't hurt you."

"They do," Philips said flatly. "They outrage me. I live in a world where a politician must fail unless he professes to believe in spooks. And when you believe in spooks you can justify anything by them. Murder. Slavery. Conversion by force."

"Charity. Liberty. Equality. Fraternity."

"Ten of mine to one of yours."

"Let's drop it," Morrison said. "Ite, missa est."

Philips grinned. "You surprise me always. Morrison the scholar."

Morrison too grinned. "Va te faire foutre." *now that is French*

Philips laughed soundlessly, a gleeful grimace, and turned solemnly to Tall Boy. "You see, Tallie, he speaks in the tongues."

Tall Boy was confused and possibly frightened, and stared at Morrison.

Morrison raised his right hand papally. "Lookoe joe oilie nanda watra befosie joe start na wagie."

They all roared. Tall Boy too.

"You come back soon," Martha said. She was leaning back against a post, her arms folded. "Nice to know you."

"Nice to know you," Morrison said. "I will come back. With pleasure."

Philips hugged her briefly. "Good-bye, old lady."

"Old lady, is it. I can still give you a better run than those girls any time."

Tall Boy looked from one to the other, delighted. His Sabbath ended early.

The motor barked, growled. Morrison looked back and waved; Martha raised a hand. Then they were winding down the hill, and in a quarter of an hour they were skimming sleepily along their own road under a high hot sun. Tall Boy, in back, shifted somehow onto his side and slept, snoring and groaning. Philips yawned.

Morrison sank into a soft, aimless, unsleeping dream.

When they slewed off the road, his knee banged that bump and he started up thinking his leg was broken, but even as he contracted in pain he saw the pale of trees and flung himself across Philips, wrenching at the wheel. Philips was awake then and stamped on the brake, and they skidded, rocked, tipped, righted, and halted sharply with the left wheels in one of the sump slashes.

Tall Boy slept.

They sat for a time under the bruising sun. Philips smoked a cigarette, thick lazy rivers of smoke pouring from his nostrils. His hand was steady. They were no more than a car's length from the trees, and after a few minutes Morrison heard a chittering and a chattering, scolding voices like the wrath of some fish-wife goddess. Morrison watched the boughs and soon saw them. He gestured and Philips nodded. They were small, with light-colored faces and nervous movements, snaky tails, the females clutching babies like any mother. Some leapt from bough to bough. Some groomed themselves or others.

"What do your friends call you?" Philips asked.

"Moe. You?"

He hesitated, a shadow of resignation in his eyes. "Just Philips." He tossed away his cigarette and vaulted out to inspect. "It is all right," he said. Then he shook Tall Boy. "Tallie," he shouted. "Lollie wants you." The monkeys fell silent.

"Oh *no,*" Tall Boy moaned from the heart.

They laughed like lunatics, out in the noonday sun. Tall Boy blinked.

Philips caught his breath. "Get up out of there. I know how you feel about working on the Sabbath, but this is an emergency."

In another hour they were home.

6

In June the near lip of the gorge was a village, with rude sheds and a parking area, stacks of lumber, coils of rope, kegs of nails, a powerful compressor, drums of petrol, and more on the way: L-shaped steel rods, cable, cement, bags of sand. The site had become part of Morrison, and he of it; he knew every hump and grade of the near side, knew the wind and the shifts of color on the earth as the sun rose and set; knew that there were owls in the fringes of forest, and woodpeckers, and shy warblers; had seen, far below, where the black water swirled white and the rocks waited like black teeth, a flock of finfoots, planing and swooping in the narrow gap, like the grebes he knew but with red bills and yellow feet. He had been over the side in a cradle of rope and knew the bare granite, its chinks and crevices, the smooth speckled gray of it.

He was alone there some of the time, and worked with half of him waiting for a sign of life across the gorge. He still wanted a sign for himself alone, and grew nervous as the road crept toward that last strip of forest; soon the gorge would be no longer his, but theirs. "We can move everything easily," Philips said.

"No. No water, for one thing."

"What are you saying? We will have to truck it in for daily use anyway. And for the concrete."

"All right. But I think it would be better for the men to live away from the work. Four miles is nothing, after all. Let them have the river at noon. A change of scene morning and night. Go home for lunch. That kind of thing."

Philips shrugged. "Whatever you say." But he knew, and soon went on, his eyes laughing: "Maybe you could find a cave in the rocks down there, and stay forever. The white hermit of Morrison's Gorge. Tourists would come and drop pennies."

Morrison laughed uneasily, because the demons of the place, who prowled at dawn and at dusk, who early roused the birds and late soothed them to silence, who whispered to him from the dark gorge, those demons were good companions. For him alone. He had come a long way to meet them, lonelier and happier with every step. Some final solitude called. Or a final mystery. To build a bridge was good; to build it to nothing was perfect. A bridge for its own sake. I claim this gorge in the name of Bernard Morrison, in perpetuity.

Across the gap, nothing. Always nothing. But they were there. There are two sides to every gorge.

Saturday evening: the sun just gone and the light fading fast, and he was alone, staring across the gorge and conscious of his own heartbeat. Feeling foolish as he mimed: sunrise, myself here, sunrise, myself here. Waving and pointing and slapping his own chest. Modern dance.

A priest gone mad, conducting insane ritual for an invisible congregation. Embarrassed, chiding himself for an idiot. Philips would bellow laughter.

He mimed again, and then stared at the shifting shadows until the light was gone.

In full darkness he boarded the truck and drove back to the deserted camp. Ramesh's radio brought him music and missionaries and garbled news of the cabinet crisis. He worried. Heard gunfire, saw his forms impounded, Goray in prison, himself deported.

Alone in the silence of a tropical night, he considered the history of Bernard Morrison, a dismal series of pathetic anecdotes. But the boy in him lived yet, and his conviction grew: he had still a day coming to him. Life owed him that. A day of wrath or a day of laughter.

He was awake at dawn, and ate mango and drank water, hurrying, and drove the four miles, shattering a cool, rosy silence, vandalizing the new day. He left his truck in the shaded grove and shambled almost timidly toward the gorge; and saw the man immediately.

It was the same man. Morrison rushed forward. The bridge of vines was up.

Morrison nodded at the man, and showed both hands, empty. It seemed the thing to do. The man was carrying a crude machete, and with it he pointed to the bridge.

Morrison was afraid, and a closer look at the bridge

did him no good. He had expected a catwalk, a floor, a walkway of some sort. He found one six-inch vine for the feet and two thinner vines for handrails. From one handrail to the other, passing beneath the heavy vine, looped about it and supporting it, were twenty or thirty thinner vines. A bridge. His throat closed. He looked down. A mistake.

But then it was all a mistake. A more terrible mistake because he could not turn back. Often enough he had been afraid, but this silent terror was new, and worse; it was self-inflicted. No one had commanded, Morrison, go to the gorge. And in the bright blush of daybreak he no longer believed that life, or destiny, or impish gods and demons, had driven him here. He saw himself driven by an invincible adolescence, by a flabby imagination nourished on illustrated tales of the frontier.

The native gestured impatiently.

Morrison cursed himself silently. He was playing at children's games, but he could not turn back. Once in his life he would follow a road to its true end.

He knew suddenly that even his terror was false. For generations men had crossed this bridge. He drew a long breath and made a joke: nothing can go wrong because I am a Master of Science.

Twenty meters. Thirty steps.

The native gestured again.

Morrison removed his sandals and slipped them into his pockets. Silly man: these people have been crossing it for years. Leaping like goats and singing.

He grasped the handrails and took one gingerly step. The bridge swayed. He shifted his weight and gave himself to the sway. Another step then, and more sway, and sweat came. With the third step he feared a wilder swing; the bridge bounced and quivered gently. The vine was rough and dry to his feet. He paused; the air here was cooler; he must not look down. Pigeon-toed, unbreathing, he went on, his palms sliding and clutching with each step, never leaving the handrails. He moved faster then, smoothly, swinging with the bridge, out and down, sliding and clutching, knees bent, balance, balance; then up, and the sway diminishing, and he took the last steps like a conqueror.

On the far lip he strode toward his host, and his knees gave way. Absolutely and without warning. He sat in the dust and smiled a friendly smile. The native edged around him at a good distance, and lowered the bridge.

God, Morrison thought: there is still the going back.

The sentry returned to stare. Morrison too stared. The sentry was naked. His body was almost hairless. He was a strong man. No scars, no tattoos. No fancy earrings or plates in the lip or bones through the nose. He might have been any man in a locker room. Except for the crude, jagged machete.

Morrison saw with shock that the man was circumcised. So was Morrison.

The native's expression never altered, and Morrison could not tell what he was thinking. The man motioned: stand up.

Morrison nodded, and put on his sandals, and rose.

The sentry stood away and waved him toward the hogback. Morrison moved forward and found a track; the man fell in behind him. They climbed the slope. The morning brightened suddenly to gold. Their track led into the brush, and then to the crest of the hill.

The view from the crest was stunning, but Morrison was given no time to marvel. A long slope of yellow grasses fell south to a wall of forest, and barely visible above the treetops was a distant range of pink mountains. Portagee mountains. They followed the track down the slope, and into the forest.

Again Morrison felt the strength in his own body, a private warmth, the sun within him. The forest murmured about them; unseen birds twittered and screeched. Bwana Tuan Sahib. He could disappear forever. Today. Right now. Never seen again. In good health but had been despondent. Hinted impotent. No life insurance. No will. Described by friends as moody. Will not be missed.

This forest was not what he had known. It was steamier. More presence. Of what? Possibilities. Vipers. Orchids.

A hot, yearning happiness almost dizzied him. Never go back. Learn the roots, the flowers. Wildfowl. Fish. Take a bride, round, greedy. Meditate. Prescribe cathartics. The holy man, and they will set bowls of rice before me. Interpret dreams. Scatter blessings.

The trail dipped into a great hollow of shade like a cavern. On the far side of the hollow, under a huge broadleaf, stood another man. Awaiting Morrison. His hair was gray and he wore a loincloth. Morrison's heart quickened. The man was fat, and stared gravely. He was not tall but seemed majestic. He might have been the lord of these trees, these shadows, these sounds; of all he surveyed.

When Morrison was six feet from him, the man laughed gleefully and said, "Vairy fuckin hallo."

His name was Bawi. "Bawi," he said, and jabbed a finger at Morrison's breast: "you Tami."

All right. Me Tami. "Tami," and Morrison nodded.

Bawi spoke to the sentry, who loped off toward the gorge, and then Bawi and Morrison were alone on the trail, sauntering homeward and gossiping. Bawi's face was broad and open, his smile ready, a free and undisciplined smile, lips stretched, teeth overwhite, cheeks popping up, eyes drowned in a fat squint, head slightly back: glee, glee, glee.

The smile said that he was no chief. He was the official greeter. Or the head poisoner; God alone knew. What was a nice fellow like Morrison doing in a place like this? He saw himself in a pot of water and Bawi rubbing two sticks together.

"You kinjo man," Bawi said with assurance.

"Yes." Whatever you say. Actually I am an American engineer. I am not Tami and not kinjo man. But then how could he be sure? They walked in single file, Bawi leading, through sparse jungle broken by sunny clearings, and downhill, amid bird-call and monkey-chatter. Bawi rolled gently as he walked, shoulder and buttock rising and falling; his eyes were downcast, as though there might be snakes or scorpions, but now and then he turned to flash that joyful pumpkin grin. Morrison imitated his strut. Perhaps he was, after all, Tami. And kinjo man. Bawi gestured languidly at a blood-red blossom: "Flar."

"Yes. Flower. Pretty."

"Pitty?"

"Beautiful."

Bawi shook his head.

"Good-looking."

Bawi grinned. "Ah lookah."

"Ah lookah."

"Dis bint ah lookah." Bawi laughed aloud. "Plenny bint. You see."

What was bint?

Insects chirred. The forest thinned soon, and after half an hour Morrison saw a dark blue gleam, and a curl of black smoke. His heart thudded; he heard it. He shook with it. Clammy hands and sudden sweat. And great thirst.

Here too there were suburbs: disused huts and a tiny goat, white and frisking. A wet smell. The huts were small and low, three posts and a grass roof. They approached a thin wall of shrubbery; a skinny dog rose from the grass and barked twice.

"Dog."

"Dog."

They breasted the shrubbery, and their journey was over.

Ten or fifteen huts stood scattered in a small clearing. At the edge of the clearing a blue creek glided lazily. Beyond the village, across the creek, the land dropped away, tangled and scrubby forest sloping off suddenly; green hills rolled to the distant mountains. Portagee side. It would be a long climb for the Portagees. The nearest Portagee town was ninety miles away, its population about three hundred; it seemed somehow closer and larger. The border was at hand, slicing through that scrubby jungle. Morrison was lonely.

The villagers were waiting, and a babble rose. Morrison tried to look agreeable but was struck blind by breasts and buttocks and hairless sexes, and cursed himself in disgust. There were faces, too, gawking at him, and he nodded regally. There were many children, all laughing; the men and women stared in silence. Some wore loincloths. The old ones. They made a lane for the travelers. At the end of the lane, sitting cross-legged before a hut, was the chief. He was much younger than Morrison. Bawi led Morrison to him and made the formal presentation: a slight bow with his hands open, palms up, one indicating Morrison and the other the chief.

The chief bowed his head twice, and Morrison did the same.

"Tami," Bawi said. "Dulani."

"Dulani," Morrison said, and bowed again.

The chief spoke in his own language.

"You here, good," Bawi said.

"Thank you."

Dulani spoke again.

"Eat?" Bawi said. "Drink? Bint?"

"Water, thank you." The sun beat at the back of his neck; he remembered then and removed the purple jockey cap.

Bawi translated, and the chief spoke again. There was a stir, and soon a young woman came to Morrison with a gourd full of water.

At her ripeness he trembled, as though he had never before seen the flesh. He closed his eyes and drank slowly, but the image of her sturdy breasts and lightly downed cleft entered him with the cool water. He drained the gourd and handed it back blindly. She went away.

The chief spoke.

Bawi grinned again, and said, "What you want here?"

Morrison stood stupidly for a time, and then returned the smile. "I don't know," he said. "I never thought of that."

After that his fears vanished. Dulani was uncertain about his last answer but remained the polite host. He instructed Bawi to show Morrison the village, and said that they would eat and drink afterward. He then retired to his hut. Women fluttered about him. He was not chiefly: a thin young man of gloomy countenance. As

Bawi and Morrison strolled among the huts, they heard
Dulani call out orders, and the crowd dispersed slowly.

"Work," Bawi said. "Plenny work."

"What work?" The huts were almost bare: earth
floors, a pot, skins, feathers.

Bawi raised one finger. "Hunt." Another finger.
"Mmmm—cassawa."

"Cassava."

"Yis sor." Another finger. "Mmmm—" It was too
much for him: he placed a hand on a grass roof and
made weaving motions.

"Yes," Morrison said.

"What dis?"

"Hut."

"Hut." He had once known the word.

"Bawi: how do you know English?"

"En'ish?"

"You talk my words."

Oh, that grin. Deafening. The sun stood still when
Bawi smiled. "Tami," he said. "Ol' Tami."

"Ol' Tami."

"Yis sor. He come much rains." With his hands he
counted twenty-two. "I show." He gestured urgently.

At the last hut, a few feet from the forest and still in
shadow, Bawi said, "Kinjo." He stooped, scuttled
within, and rooted in a corner. Morrison thought he saw
canvas and grommets, a buckle. Bawi popped out. He
was wriggling into a khaki shirt, and Morrison saw an
inverted chevron on either sleeve.

"Tommy," Morrison said.

"Tami." Bawi grinned again. "Oh fine Tami. Vairy fuckin fine Tami."

"Tommy stay here?"

"Tami here one rain. Rain go, he go."

"Where he go?"

"Portagee side." Bawi waved southward.

A deserter. "He come back?"

Bawi shook his head sadly, and said something that Morrison could not understand, but not in the chief's language. Portuguese, he realized suddenly.

"You talk Portagee?"

"Oh yis sor. You talk Portagee?"

"No. How come you talk Portagee?"

"Talk Portagee fine,' Bawi said. "T'ree rain, Portagee come. T'ree rain, come back. T'ree rain, t'ree rain, Portagee come. I show."

Their audience was gathering again; they trailed a retinue. Morrison could look at them now; it was a perfectly normal day in a perfectly normal year and he was paying a call on some perfectly normal old friends. He waved. Children giggled. The boys were not circumcised; the men were. Painful. There were old women he remembered from magazines, with breasts like wattles.

But Bawi tugged him along, and at another hut—they were all alike to Morrison—he scuttled again and emerged with a small roll of white cloth. "Portagee." It was ordinary thin cotton. He replaced it and pushed Morrison forward. "I show."

At Dulani's hut he squatted, and his finger traced

whorls in the dust as he chattered. Dulani grunted and nodded wearily and spoke to a woman, who slipped away. Morrison watched her go; she was young. Dulani's eyes were cloudy. He did not look; he peered.

"Soon," Bawi said.

So Morrison squatted beside him, hunkered down with his behind on his heels, and traced letters in the same dust until his civilized arches gave way. He rocked back on his heels then and stood up. But the woman was back, and with her an old man in a cotton cloth, not merely a loincloth but draped about his middle like a kirtle or whatever it was that Gandhi wore.

"Malani," Bawi said, rising. "Him pop," pointing at Dulani and doubtless meaning that the chief was the old man's son, which did not seem right, but Morrison was far from home and disinclined to pry.

Morrison bowed, and the old man bowed. Then from a fold of his diaper he drew a knife.

It was a jackknife, well cared for, with three blades: the knife-blade, a nail-file and bottle-opener, and a corkscrew. Morrison was at ease now and feeling rather superior to these interesting folk, so he thought of Malani as the sommelier.

"Good knife," he said.

"Knife," Bawi said happily, remembering, and repeated it to Dulani.

Malani nodded, as if in relief: "Knife," he said.

"What is a knife in your talk?"

"Urka," Bawi said. Or Ruka. R'ka. He made a strange click deep in his throat and belched forth an *r*.

"What is water in your talk?"

"La."

La. How right. La.

"Why does Malani keep the knife? Why not Bawi?"

Bawi smiled, this time gently and with admiration. "Malani make pig, make dog, make—" He squatted again and grimaced, waved, chittered, picked at his armpits. The villagers chuckled and giggled.

"Monkey," Morrison said.

"Mon-key."

They all practiced, in a general murmur.

"You show me."

They turned away, but Morrison remembered his manners. "Tell Dulani thank you."

Dulani nodded again without interest. Bawi spoke and they moved off, cortege and all.

Malani's hut was at the riverbank. Some of the children left them to slide and plunge, like otters playing. Bawi and Morrison squatted again while Malani puttered in the shade. The sun was higher; another brazen day.

Malani ranged three pieces before them: a pig and a dog and a monkey, in grainy gray wood. They were badly proportioned and static, just a pig and a dog and a monkey, not doing anything, not rooting or sniffing or scratching, but recognizable.

Bawi beamed. Malani was properly withdrawn; indifferent; preoccupied.

"They're beautiful," Morrison said. "Very good-looking."

Bawi rattled the compliment to Malani, who bowed, cast his eyes down, and smirked slightly in the manner of the lionized artist, so perfect in his condescending thanks to a negligible critic that Morrison had to repress a bray.

"Tell Malani thank you."

Bawi did so, and they took gracious leave of the master.

"What do you give the Portagee?"

Bawi did not understand.

"The Portagee gives you knife. What do you give him?"

Still unclear, Bawi offered, "Eat. Drink. Plenny bint."

Bint again. So bint was food and drink.

"Eat, drink now," Bawi said. "You come."

Morrison turned to inspect their following, twenty or so, braving the sun for him. Three were men, impassive. Half were children, who tittered trying to hide behind one another. The old women shushed them. Four or five were young women, and it was difficult not to stare. There was much to stare at, and it was somehow handsomer than he had ever seen, stronger, healthier, directed frankly at him, not pale and imprisoned and gouged by straps. Overpowering. The faces were open black faces, clear eyes and wide nostrils, small ears, the hair only a frizz. They stared back at him. He wanted momentarily to take them and go to a dark place; but he could be of no use to them, and they were not born for dark places. He was perturbed, assaulted, made small; they called to him and shamed him.

Bawi grinned. He knew. "Bint," he said.

"Let's go," Morrison said, and turned away.

Dulani was a sick man. Morrison saw that in his lethargy, his dim sight, his indifference. When he needed a gourd, or a broad leaf, he spoke, and one of his women placed it directly before him, and in reaching he groped. Morrison wondered how much of Bawi's translation was truth and how much fiction; how much Dulani and how much Bawi.

"What you want here?" Bawi asked again.

They were drinking water from gourds and eating breadfruit. Their bowls were gourds; leaves their plates. The same young woman served Morrison, kneeling to place the gourd before him, and the sunny, musky smell of her breasts was an ache inside him.

"I wanted to know the men on this side."

Bawi understood, and was pleased. He made the announcement, and a murmur answered. "What you make?" He gestured loosely toward the gorge.

Morrison sipped at the water, and rushed in: "A new bridge."

Bawi shook his head.

"To cross." With his hands Morrison outlined a gorge, deep, deep, with one finger arched a bridge across the top. Then he drew it in the dust.

"Ah." With alarm; Bawi was alert now. "You talk what?"

"Bridge," Morrison said again. "Big bridge. Good bridge. Walk on like this." With the flat of his hand he pounded the earth. "Many men walk together, same time." He showed Bawi the fingers of both hands and pointed to many of the villagers. "All on bridge. Big bridge."

Bawi explained that. Silence followed. Morrison saw the pot of hot water again.

"Tami come?"

"No. No more Tami. Man like Bawi come. Black man."

"Come do what?"

Morrison shook his head. "Come do nothing. Come give knife. Many things."

He shut up then, chilled suddenly by the sharp wind of untruth. In this village were no lies, he believed, and he could not know what the bridge would bring.

Bawi said gloomily, "Hut here." His arm swept a half circle. "All time hut here. Bawi pop hut here. Pop pop. Pop pop *pop.*"

"All time pop."

"No, no. Ol' ol' pop come here." He pointed. "You come. Same you come."

"What for ol' ol' pop come here?" The talk seemed natural now. He would some day tell Devoe, "Make bridge all done. You give Moe much money."

"Mmmmm." Bawi's search for words was agonizing. His mind strained back twenty-two years. He waved again toward the gorge, the country itself, the capital. "Tami come. Too much Tami. Bad Tami. Ol' ol' pop come here. All pop come. No bad Tami here."

Dulani spoke.

Bawi said, "Good here. La. Waw-da. No, mmm, gun. No Tami. Much cassawa. Much pig. No want much man here."

"Bawi." Morrison too struggled with the vocabulary. "This side good man. Black man like Bawi. Portagee side maybe bad man. Maybe bad man come here. Take all. No good. Then good man come help Bawi push 'em back." He gestured violently.

"Portagee man not bad," Bawi said flatly.

"One rain, two rain, ten rain," all Morrison's fingers fanlike, "maybe Portagee man bad."

Bawi was obviously unimpressed. After a moment he said, "Bad. Bad. Bad."

There were no mass farewells. By noon, when Morrison started back to the gorge, most of the village was bathing in the stream; a formal and customary respite, he gathered. Men, and women, and children bathed in separate groups. They rubbed themselves with sand. The children ducked and spouted. Morrison was about to ask if this was a ceremony for Sundays, but remembered that there were no Sundays.

He pointed. "All time?"

"Sun here," Bawi's arm vertical, "come wawda."

"Every day."

Bawi smiled as memory blossomed. "Ever' day, sun here, come wawda."

"Me too," Morrison said.

"You want come wawda now?"

"No. I'll go on now."

"You come back?"

"Yes."

"Good," Bawi said, and they set out for the gorge.

Along this same trail, twenty-two years before, had come Old Tommy, Lance Corporal Anonymous, fabled in song and story as the Unknown Deserter, pride and idol of millions; he had *had* this bloody war and would no longer be a number. Or even a name. From the dim artificial light of a Birmingham slum and a sluggish troopship and a sweat-stinking barracks he had passed this way to the black incandescence of a border village, and on then to the world, born again. Morrison saw a short, tough street rat, dropping aitches, joking indecently, taking charge. The magic cigarette lighter. A stolen pistol. Now owning a saloon in Rio de Janeiro or Lourenço Marques or Singapore. I am that I am. Old Tommy. Dead and resurrected. Twice-born. Hail!

"This Old Tommy," he said.

Bawi paused.

"Old Tommy have another name? You call him another word?"

"No no. Ol' Tami, him."

Lost. There would be records. Sir: We are searching for a lance corporal last seen snipping the equator with a stolen pair of government-issue wire-cutters. He has come into a small legacy. Please advise. TOMMY: COME BACK. ALL IS FORGIVEN. UNCLE MALANI NEEDS YOU IN THE BUSINESS. No questions asked.

No. Old Tommy would not like that. It was odd to

think that any Englishman over forty—a clerk in a bowler in Cheapside, or the drunken beachcomber of New Providence—might be Old Tommy. He might even have gone back to Birmingham, and be a factory hand right now, this moment. Keeping the wogs out of the union. Or—

"Old Tommy white man or black man?"

Bawi grinned that sunrise grin and laughed aloud. "Whi' man. No Tami black man. No Tami black man." His laughter melted to a giggle, and Morrison saw by his eyes that he was composing the anecdote. He will tell them at the sunset meal, Morrison thought, and it will go down to the sons and the sons' sons. "With the white man I was walking, where the grass turns yellow at the great red hill, and he was talking, and he talked of *black soldiers*." How they would laugh and shout! And the story would never fail. On dull evenings one man would nudge another and say, "Let's see if we can get Bawi to tell that story about the crazy white man and the black soldiers."

It was all rather sad.

They made ceremonious farewells at the bridge, and Morrison crossed with no difficulty. The two black men lowered the bridge, and waved, and vanished into the bush. Morrison drove back to camp, and sat in the wawda a while, and slept naked in a hammock.

Philips found him there at about four.

"Welcome home," Morrison said sleepily. "A good weekend?"

"The usual. Martha sends regards."

"Thank you. I don't see any bruises."

"It was really very quiet," Philips said. "As I assume it was here."

"It was. I pondered the words of Ramesh and found serenity."

"Oh," Philips said. "Your crane has arrived."

7

The port was a marvel of disorder. For two miles the river was barely visible from the road, cut off by a string of warehouses and sheds. The road swarmed: trucks, donkeys, dockers, on the landward side shops and markets; thousands of men, women and children toting, shouting, buying, selling. A white man, mustachioed, in a pith helmet: Morrison stared unbelieving. Twice, grade crossings. They pushed along in low gear, declining manslaughter time and again; before them and behind them were trucks and wagons enduring the same slow pilgrimage. Their goal was government wharf number one, the last of the line and the deepest anchorage. The crowd thinned toward the end, and they drove the last half mile in second gear. Tall Boy was strangely courteous, gesturing in courtly fashion at pedestrians, clucking at menaced fowl, laughing with children. Just before the sea-wall they turned left, and there was the mouth of the muddy river, a hundred yards off, and when they had rounded the sheds and were on the waterfront itself, Morrison saw the straight line of railroad tracks, and freights and engines, run-

ning back the full two miles. And at that too he caught
his breath: ten or a dozen freighters of all sizes, and the
tracks and cars, and longshoremen shuttling and chant-
ing, and the sheds of odd shapes, and trucks and jeeps,
and the smell of the river, of oil, of wood, all that in the
hot yellow morning light—why should that be less
beautiful than a sunset, or mist at dawn on a mountain
stream? It was not less beautiful. More beautiful, perhaps, because it was human. Men, accomplishing. Taking sun, wood, muscle, steel, human need, and making
of them a manscape in dull browns and bright yellows
and gleaming silver-whites.

The Xenophon rode low in the water before them, a
small Liberian flag hanging limp astern. Her forward
hatches were open and booms and cables strained; the
air was thick with whirrings and groanings and click-
ings. A small, cocky, bright-red automobile hung high,
swaying and then still, and began its descent. Two more
like it stood shaded by a wooden overhang. Clean
wooden crates filled a corner of the vast shed.

Tall Boy backed into the shade and they stepped out
and stretched. "How long it take to get her off?"

"All day," Morrison said. "So you take it easy. That's
fifty tons, don't forget. Will there be a telephone here?"

"Oh yes. Telephones all up and down here."

"Good. Stick around. I'll try to find Goray."

Tall Boy squinted out at the light, and found a post
to lean against. He cocked his fez and examined the
scene carefully, his eyes shifting and his mind absorb-
ing, and then he concentrated on the hoists and the man

in a small box who was making them work. Morrison
liked him. Morrison wanted to see that broad, open face
when they gave him his crane.

Goray was in the dockmaster's office on the second
floor of the shed. When Morrison came in, Goray
grinned mischievously and roared welcome. His shirt
was scarlet today, and a broad-brimmed Panama hat
gave him an overseer's air. "Engineer Morrison! How
delightful! This is Dockmaster Hartog. I am afraid we
have no banana brandy."

Morrison shook hands with Hartog, a skinny man all
in white, and then with Goray. "I can still taste the last
bottle."

Goray heaved and rippled, laughing. The room was
musty and cool.

"Everything is in order," Hartog said.

"Yes," Goray said. "This is quite a day. I cannot wait
to see this machine."

"Neither can I. Or to make it work. It's been a long
trip, and things go wrong. How soon will they have it
off?"

"You must ask the captain, or the master of cargo.
But the clearance is here, thanks to Mister Hartog." He
waved a sheaf of papers, and slipped them into a folder
as Hartog smiled. A cock crowed outside, close by, star-
tling, and they all laughed.

"Fanfare," Goray said emphatically. "A good sign."

"Is there a phone? May I call my office? I've ordered
a truck for the boom."

Goray was interested. "You cannot leave it on the
crane?"

"Not at forty miles an hour. It's long and heavy, you know. We'd tip at the first curve."

"Ah. And on the job?"

"Maximum speed five miles an hour on the job. Better still, three."

"I see, I see." To Hartog he bubbled, "Technology, my friend. Salvation in a homicidal world. Nuclear energy, next. Power-plants. Our great need."

"And stability."

Goray blinked.

"General Ros." Morrison was showing off.

Goray's face told him not to pursue it. Of course. He felt foolish.

"Anyway, is there a phone?"

"There is a telephone downstairs," Hartog said. "On the street side."

"Then you'll excuse me."

"Yes, yes, go ahead." Goray waved him off. "I shall join you shortly."

"My pleasure," Hartog said, and they shook hands again.

Downstairs the smell of hides was stupefying. Bales of hides. Rows of bales of hides. Morrison did not envy the longshoremen, or even the crew of the Xenophon. Bags of coffee, then, much better, and rice. Timber. A huge crate labeled WORKS OF ART bearing an address in London. Bags of sugar: he stepped closer to sniff, but backed away quickly: bees swarmed.

Utu answered, and Morrison instructed him to have the truck there at noon. Two drivers, and they must plan to spend the night at the camp. And the small crane should leave immediately. Utu was crisp and confident: it would be done.

"One more thing, sir."

"What is it?"

"We have been wondering, the three of us, if . . . if we might, ah, come to see the unloading."

Behind the casual words, perhaps in that brief hesitation, was an intensity that shocked Morrison; an intensity not heard, not even felt in an ordinary way, but registering violently upon some new sense, unused and unsuspected before now.

"Yes." Morrison was flustered. "Yes, sure. Take a half holiday. Come down after lunch."

"Oh, thank you! Thank you, sir, thank you!"

"Well, sure," he said. "See you later." He hung up.

Good God! One little old fifty-ton crane!

And yet he understood.

Goray and he boarded the Xenophon and were led to her captain, a man of forty or so, unlined and cheerful and blond, who glanced briefly at the clearances and poured three tots of whisky and sent for his chief mate, a man of thirty or so, also unlined and cheerful and blond, who said that the boom would come off at one, the carrier by three, and the upper cab by five. The cables were off already, and there had been no damage whatsoever, not a scratch, a smooth crossing. A crate of parts was on the dock.

"Thank God," Morrison said.

"I thank you in the name of the government." Goray

raised his glass. "With whisky before luncheon. That is a most valuable machine."

"It's a pretty one, too," the chief mate said. "I'd join you, there, but I'm working. Cheers anyway. The kind of machine you get fond of."

"Just get it off in one piece," the captain said.

"Will do," he said. "Where do we put it?"

"There'll be a truck here for the boom," Morrison said. "A forty-foot flat trailer. Just drop it gently, the long way, the inserts too. If you could get that crate of parts on afterward I'd appreciate it."

The chief mate said, "No sweat."

The captain's cabin was like a room at a motel. There was even a print of Old Faithful. But the maple chairs were bolted to the floor.

"Drop the upper cab on the carrier. There's a hole in the bottom, and a post in the carrier that goes up through the hole. I'll position it for you."

The chief mate said warily, "You know about this kind of work?"

"No. But I'm an engineer, and I know this machine. I won't touch anything. Or you can come down and do it."

"We'll do it together," the young man said agreeably.

"Good. Then I'll set the flanges and we'll be off your dock in half an hour."

"Lovely," the young man said.

"How do you unload the carrier?"

The captain was bored. Goray was bright-eyed and alert.

"We drive it right down a ramp." The chief mate smiled. "Same ramp we drove it up."

"Good old American know-how," Morrison said.

"Yes sir," the chief mate said with vigor. "That Liberian flag didn't fool you for a minute. What are you going to do with this machine, anyway?"

"Build a bridge," Morrison said.

"Great," the chief mate said, and then, "Where you from?" and that killed the next few minutes, and then Morrison towed off a reluctant Goray and went to find Tall Boy.

Tall Boy stood among sweaty dockers, and was offering cigarettes. The dockers wore ragged pants and nothing else. Some bore hooks and some shoulder-pads. "Oh, that is a bridge," Tall Boy was saying. "People going to come out there just to *look* at that bridge."

Goray and Morrison lingered in the shade and did not interrupt. From here, at the bows, they could see the river, a mile and more across, sluggish, brown, implacable; and a barge, and half a dozen dugouts, pirogues, one deep under coconuts. The far shore was surprisingly bare: one wooden building, many shacks, a fringe of palms. The land lay flat along the coast, and there was no forest, only a long flat sweep of green and dun to the far horizon. "There is a ferry," Goray said, "and a road, for about thirty miles, to a settlement called Himmel's Creek. In between, a few farms."

"I'm sorry I mentioned Ros. That was stupid."

Goray shrugged. "It was only that we do not know

how Hartog feels. A certain discretion is valuable."

"Yes. How are things? Politically, I mean. The radio scares us and then says everything is all right."

"Yes. Officially, all is well. But I worry. It is so easy, you see, when you have a general to give orders. Your George Washington was not the father of his country because he conceived it, but because he *took care* of things. The children came to him with their troubles and he resolved them. Though I will admit that he was an unusual man. In spite of his slaves. A Yorkshireman, I believe. With big feet. Do you know what I have never understood about your country?"

"No. But it's nice of you to admit there's something."

"Touché." Goray was genuinely delighted. "I have never understood how, with so much power to be grabbed, your early politicians declined it. Not merely Washington refusing the monarchy; but all of them so busy making a good country that they forgot to assure themselves lifetime jobs, and salt monopolies, and whole counties."

"They'd just rebelled against all that."

Goray was astonished. "My dear fellow. You cannot be so naïve. Name one other—any other, anywhere, any time—group of revolutionaries who did not immediately assume the privileges of the deposed."

"I'm afraid I don't know that much history," Morrison said. "I wish I did. You and Philips make me feel illiterate."

"We don't mean to." Goray smiled. "It is desperation

on our part. There is so much to learn—so much being forced upon us so suddenly—that the few of us who
can read and write are permanently drunk with knowl-
edge. Most of it, I must say, useless. This machine, now
—that impresses me."

"Me too. I don't know how a machine can make a
man so happy, but when they told me it was undam-
aged—"

"I noticed," Goray said. "I felt somewhat the same.
The life of the government depends not on intentions
but on accomplishment. On other things too, maneuvering and deals and so forth. But also accomplishment.
Statistics. So much more rice grown. So many miles of
road put down. So many telephones. Housing, bridges,
hospitals. If we slacken, the people will feel cheated and
will fall in behind some general—like Ros—who will
tell them to win the world's respect by being strong;
even making war. Horrible. That man is the real savage."

"Well, the bridge will be a good one," Morrison said.
"You can promise them that. It will also be one of the
most beautiful bridges in the world." Morrison nodded
seriously. "In the world. Tall Boy is right: people will
come to see it. And it took no genius. Only technique."

"Good." Goray's smile was faintly like Bawi's; a pale
copy. "Maybe it will keep us in power for another week
or two."

Morrison laughed. "My boss told me to stay out of
politics."

Goray arched in glee, eyes and mouth wide. "You

were—wait, wait, there is an American phrase." Finger raised, eyes glittering behind his glasses, he sought. "Yes! You were *arse-deep* in politics the moment you landed."

They laughed together, and Goray slapped him on the back. Tall Boy heard them, and broke away from the dockers.

"Tall Boy," Morrison said. "This is Mister Goray."

"Albert Goray." He shook hands with Tall Boy, who was uneasily respectful and tipped the fez with his left hand.

"Tall Boy is the heavy machinery man," Morrison said. "The best in the country. This crane is for him."

"Ah." Goray bowed slightly. "You are an important man, Tall Boy. Take care of your toy."

"I will."

"We'll have it on the road by six," Morrison said. "We'll take it to Serpa's tonight. He has that big lot. We'll stay at the hotel and start out in the morning. *If* nothing bad happens."

"I could sleep in the crane," Tall Boy said.

"Nobody's going to make off with it. There's only one man in the country who knows how to run it."

"You," Goray said.

"Me. By tomorrow night, me and Tall Boy."

Tall Boy took on the look of a new father. "Lord Jesus," he said.

"You are a Christian?" Goray asked.

"Yes sir. You, sir?"

"No," Goray said mournfully. "I am a politician."

Then he grinned his quick grin and said, "Let us go and eat."

They ate rice and beef and peppers and shards of co-conut, all heated up in one pot, and drank tea. When they returned to the dock, the truck was there, the long flat-bed trailer, and there too were Utu and Isaacson and Vieira-Souza, all in white, short sleeves, no hats, like cricketers at the tea-break, but they were drinking beer from bottles. They greeted Morrison almost timidly, and he introduced them to Goray, whom it seemed they had met, and there was nothing to do but stand in the shade and chat.

After a while a hatch opened, and blocks swung and cables stretched and twanged. The chief mate joined them, sweating through his khaki shirt, and Morrison presented him. "Why don't you take off your shirt?"

"Company rule," the chief mate said blithely. "Tell the men from the boys," meaning nothing special, but he did not see the look that crossed five faces, and Morrison did.

A monstrous lattice of steel emerged from the hatch. Their boom. The sun danced off it in a hundred blinding glints.

"Where do you want the truck?"

"Right where it is," the chief mate said. "We took care of all that while you were gone."

Morrison asked Utu, "Where are the drivers?"

"Gone to buy a drink," Utu said, and Morrison was so taken with the music of "byee ah dreenk" that he was almost not angry.

"Find them," Morrison said. "Right now. And tell them to lay off the drink until they reach camp tonight."

"Yes. Yes sir," Utu said, frightened, not knowing what it cost Morrison to issue an angry order.

Their boom hung high, and swung toward them, drifting and silver-black against the deep yellow sky. It passed across the sun. Morrison was dazzled, and looked down at the chief mate, who stood beside the trailer semaphoring. The boom hung still, then lower, lower, lower; the mate and his men laid guiding hands upon it, and shifted their feet. The mate waved again, and the boom settled gently on six inches of matting. The men disengaged the cables. Morrison wiped his brow.

Tall Boy poked him. "How we get that on the crane?" he worried.

Morrison put an arm around his shoulders. The boom was down, and safe. "Another crane. A small one. It went out this morning. Maybe the same one you had at Gimbo."

"That was ten ton," Tall Boy said. "You know about Gimbo?"

"Yes."

"That was funny," Tall Boy said.

"Okay, gentlemen," Morrison said. "Show's over for now. Nothing more till about three." The chief mate came laughing up. "Good work," Morrison said. "Thanks."

"Service with a smile," he said. "Call again." An ass, Morrison decided.

Two hours later the hull swung open amidships and became a ramp. The boom, the inserts, the crate of parts were gone, in the care of Morrison's tippling drivers, who had submitted indifferently to his amateurish reprimand and accepted somewhat more gracefully his promise of abundant beer at the end of the line. Which left the six of them loitering, smoking, watching other men work, dodging the sun; yawning. When the ramp came down, Tall Boy laid a huge hand on Morrison's shoulder, and Goray flashed him a comical glance of mock terror, and the other three fell silent and gawked.

The chief mate was not an ass. He urged her out at a mile an hour, swung her right at the moment Morrison would have chosen, and brought her to a stop far down the dock, at the bows, with plenty of room to back her into place for the upper cab. He ordered the ramp up, and waited, and only when the dock was clear came to Morrison and asked, smiling, brisk and smug, if he wanted to take over.

"Yes," Morrison said. "Come on, Tall Boy. First lesson."

They scrambled aboard. It was not much of a lesson because the carrier was driven much like any truck, but it was twenty-five feet long and weighed twenty-four tons and was not altogether child's play. Tall Boy whispered to himself. Morrison backed with great care. He set the brakes, cut the motor, dropped the keys into his shirt pocket and buttoned the flap. "The driving is just oiler's work," he said. "The real work is in the cab."

Tall Boy nodded; he knew.

Their three engineers stood like bridesmaids as they descended, and Goray insisted on an examination of the dashboard. He inspected the wheels and the platform and pronounced himself pleased. Morrison was meanwhile checking the oil and water. Lookoe joe oilie nanda watra befosie joe start na wagie. Yes sir.

And so it went: a perfect day. The upper cab emerged as promised, toward five, and they worried some more because it was immense, and full of beautifully complicated mechanisms; one good jolt would have drawn hot tears and keening sobs from all of them. But the mate knew his job, and won their hearts, setting down thirteen tons like a fisherman dropping a fly on a leaf. Morrison felt for a moment what he had felt often before, that any man who did his job well was a man to like; and then remembered General Ros, who was presumably doing his job well and whom he did not think he would like at all. A fleeting thought. He thanked the young man. Then he went aboard and thanked the captain. Then he thanked Goray. Then his three engineers thanked him. Morrison had Tall Boy give them the keys to the Land-Rover, and said he wanted one of them to run it out to the camp tomorrow and hitch a ride back on the flat-bed. They went away squabbling. "Utu," Morrison said. "One dollar."

"A bet," Tall Boy said. "Isaacson wins. He been longer with the company."

Before Goray left he said, "A good day's work. The bridge is important. I told you that."

"Yes. To me too. You'll get a beauty. Just stay in office a while, will you?"

"Oh yes," Goray said. "There is much to be done after the bridge." He was teasing solemnly.

"I know. Farms. Food. Timber. People who can hope to live past thirty."

"Oh well," Goray said. "That is exaggerated, you know. Those averages include infant mortality, which is high." Everything at his fingertips; Morrison marveled. "If a man reaches the age of ten here he can expect to see sixty." Then his eyes went blank, and a wry smile plucked at his lips: "That is, if he wants to."

So Morrison and Tall Boy proceeded in stately array toward the capital, the sun vanishing behind them and pedestrians paying homage before them, staring, clumps of them turning like sunflowers at the smooth and almost silent approach of this new monster; but a peaceful monster, and it seemed to Morrison that they sensed its benevolence and welcomed it. Romance, he supposed, deriding himself gently; and yet, and yet. The man who has never driven a fifty-ton crane through a tropical capital at nightfall has no right to laugh. Tropical capitals exist only in dreams, anyway, and when you are there you do too; the overpowering scent of flowers at twilight in an unrelieved slum, and then you turn a corner and the whole next block is one flaming flower-market, and a barefoot girl in a yellow dress lights the dusk with her smile, and her arms are full of blue and red blossoms. Then the next block is an out-

house, and the next a swamp of alcohol, and then an il-
luminated sign blares CHARLIE CHAPLIN, or a brightly
lit black dummy stands in the window of a department
store sporting a set of tails. With a medal in the lapel,
and if you come closer the medal reads JORROCKS
HUNT CLUB. And the night closes in, lamps glow,
music floats and twangs. A policeman stops traffic for
you, and salutes your passage. Tall Boy answers the
salute. And when you arrive at Serpa's, the darkness
envelops you and only your own beams light the way,
and it is best that they be bright.

And then silence, and stars, until Tall Boy turned to
him and said, "I think I ought to sleep here, boss. I really
do."

"No. We're going to eat some good steaks and drink
all the beer we can hold, and sleep like babies."

"Very good," he said. "Yes, very good. Eh, one thing,
boss."

"What's that?"

"Will they let me in this hotel?"

Not since he came here had Morrison been so angry.
"For Christ's sake, Tallie!" Morrison could have throt-
tled him. "This is *your country!*"

"Oh, no, boss," Tall Boy soothed him. "No, no, no,"
and set a hand on his shoulder again, "I just meant I
got no necktie," and patted him.

And now who was the ass?

In the morning Morrison stopped off to buy half a
dozen machetes, and said that he wanted them wrapped,

any sort of package, which astounded the wizened, ferrety Hindu in his open wooden stall. So Morrison took them as they were and went to buy a gunny sack. At Serpa's he hid them under the driver's seat. Serpa was all over the crane, nodding and muttering, tugging at his mustache—he looked like a lover in an Italian opera—and calling on his gods. "Beautiful, beautiful! Some machine! Some machine! Capital!"

"It's a good one," Morrison said. "Hey, Serpa. Tell me something."

"Anything, Mister Morrison. Serpa is at your service." He even bowed.

"You really used the best? All the way through? Absolutely the best?"

"Mister Morrison," he said sadly, as if Morrison had questioned his piety. "Mister Morrison." He was a solid man, and dark, and might have spent much time in the field. That was unreasonably reassuring. "If this bridge was my own, my own private bridge, the Manoel Serpa bridge, I could not have found one kilo of material better than what I use here. For you. Listen." He drew nearer; his eyes darted. "Now that we are a country if the material is bad you know what happens?"

"What?"

"They put Serpa in jail. You ever been to jail in a hot country, Mister Morrison?"

"Never been to jail at all," Morrison said apologetically.

"Believe me, Mister Morrison," Serpa said. "You just believe me."

"I trust you absolutely," Morrison said.

And they shook hands, and Serpa fluttered fingers at Tall Boy, and Morrison locked his door and turned the key.

Tall Boy understood the truck immediately, and they were not five miles outside the capital when Morrison yielded to him. "Forty. Never, under any circumstances, more than forty. Keep her at thirty for a while. Get the feel."

After a time Tall Boy asked about "those things down below go in and out. They *look* like they go in and out."

"They do. They're hydraulic outriggers. You know what hydraulic is?"

"Fluid in the cylinder," Tall Boy said, offended. "Pressure."

"They keep you from tipping," Morrison said.

"Tall Boy will not tip."

"That's not the way to think about it. You ought to worry about tipping. Look: that boom can extend to a hundred and fifty feet. That's a long boom. You can hold sixteen tons with it. Sixteen tons, Tall Boy. That's a lot of load. That's thirty-two thousand pounds. What's the most you ever lifted?"

"Two ton," Tall Boy said grudgingly. "A long girder."

"There," Morrison said. "You think about this. With this you can hold sixteen tons, but only in a radius of thirty-five feet. Now suppose you have that swinging and it comes to the corner, the weak spot, and all of a sudden it's out there forty feet."

"I got it," Tall Boy said. "Outriggers. I understand. I never had one so big before."

"Right. You won't have to handle anything near sixteen tons. But you have to know the limits. As the weight goes down, the radius grows longer. I have tables here." He hesitated. "Can you read and write?"

"I read some," Tall Boy said. "Numbers okay. And anything on a machine. Ig-ni-tion. Brake. Overdrive. And I can write my name. Print. Tall Boy. T-a-l-l-b-o-y."

"We'll go over the tables together. You ought to learn to read and write."

"Not much need."

"Just the same."

"Well why then?"

They had a long day ahead of them, so Morrison slumped and crossed his legs comfortably and told him. He felt silly preaching, and could not remember just where he had learned this, but it was a thing he had been taught and had never forgotten. "Well. In some countries you have two kinds of people. The ones who can read and write and never do any work with their hands, and the ones who work with their hands and never learn to read and write. And it doesn't take long before the first ones decide not to let the second ones even learn, and right there you get masters and slaves. Happened in many places a long time ago. China. Black countries, right here, some of your neighbors. Other places it didn't happen because there were enough men who learned to do both. Maybe there were not so

many people to start with, so some men had to do two
jobs. So there were men who could read and write and
weren't too proud to work, and men who worked and
had the chance to learn more. That's what a foreman is,
Tall Boy. A sergeant. A gang boss. An independent
farmer. That's what an independent country is, when
you think about it. Anyway the more people can do both,
the better for the country. Where I live you have to go
to school until your seventeenth birthday."

"Who pays for that?"

"Taxes."

"Who pays taxes?"

"Everybody. Almost everybody. Rich people get
around it."

Tall Boy grinned. "I pay no taxes, boss. That make
me a rich man."

"You will," Morrison said. "Believe me. And if there's
nobody around who can read and write, who's going
to do the arguing? Fight the tax collector?"

Tall Boy fell glum.

"Cheer up," Morrison said. "It isn't hard. You have a
good start. And then you can read the Bible."

"I thought of that. Many times I wanted to read in
the Bible. They say some hot stories in the Bible."

Morrison reproved him roundly.

They rolled in well after noon. The camp was deserted
—Morrison saw the Land-Rover, and the trailer with
the boom, and the small crane—so Tall Boy beat on
the horn half a dozen times and then held it down. Mor-

rison barely had time to dash to his trailer with the machetes. Shortly men raced out of the forest, and shouted when they saw, and ringed the crane, pounding the carrier and kicking all twelve tires—universal!— and caressing the white metal of the cab. Philips and Ramesh were the last out, and when Philips saw what was happening he ran forward and flung the men away, roaring and cursing. They stood silent. They could hear him breathing. His fists were clenched against his thighs.

"What the hell," Morrison said gently. "They just wanted to see the new machine."

"Yes," Philips drawled, "and snap off a handle. Or jam a switch. Or piss in the engine to cool it."

"Well." Morrison was back on the carrier, looking down at him, and made the most of it. "This is a new Philips."

There was no humbling him. "No. This is the same Philips. It is a new machine, though. And you have not seen what can happen."

"Tall Boy," Morrison said, "take it into the shade. Ramesh, can we get something to eat and drink? It's been a long morning."

"Immediately," Ramesh said. "Jacob!"

Philips and Morrison walked quietly to the trailers. "You'd better explain," Morrison said.

"It is the same old story," Philips said. "We had irrigation pumps inland—at an experimental station, mind you—and they were gone in a month. Why? No one oiled them. Why? Because there was no oil. Why?

Because the appropriation for pumps included no money for oil. Why? Because no one thought of it."

"All right. But they want to look. We told them they'd work better if they knew more. Let them. Stay with them if necessary. You can't treat them like that."

"Sometimes you have to," Philips said.

"Not on my job."

And then Philips said, as Morrison had known he would, "You are the boss."

They spent a hot afternoon rigging the boom, and by five no one was talking to anyone else. Only Tall Boy chuckled. Isaacson had returned the Land-Rover, so after they had sent back the crane, and the truck, and Isaacson with it, Morrison paid Tall Boy his dollar. He wanted no other man's company—Philips had blasted a perfectly fine day—so on a quick impulse he asked Tall Boy to the trailer for a bottle of beer. Philips stiffened even more.

"Sergeants too," was all Morrison said.

Before Tall Boy went off to dunk himself at dusk, he asked, "Boss, you remember what you said about foremen? Well what kind of country you got when everybody is a foreman?"

"I never thought about that," Morrison said. "But I will."

8

"Oooh," Bawi breathed, and the others murmured "Aaaah." Dulani craned forward blinking, and spoke, and smiled, revealing sparse brown teeth.

The shadows were long and cool; morning sun sparked off the blue steel machetes. Morrison was remembering the gunny sack, heavy on his back, and the rope biting his shoulders, and the bridge of vines swaying, and his hands sweaty. And the trembling afterward.

Bawi dropped to his knees before Morrison, touched the earth with his forehead, and rose to say, "Dulani say tank. All man say tank. Bawi say tank. Dis knife—" He shook his head; words were inadequate. "Dis knife *good.*"

"Yes." Morrison nodded uncomfortably. "Good knife. Okay. No more tank."

Dulani spoke again, and his women fanned him. He went on talking, and men stepped forward. Five of them. They were a muscular crew. But one of them had a cloudy eye like Dulani's, and another a withered arm, and a third no scrotum, only a flap of papery skin. Morrison winced.

Gravely Bawi presented the machetes; gravely the men accepted. The sixth he kept. Solemnities at an end, he grinned. "Much pig."

"Good."

"What you want?"

"Want?"

"You give knife. What you want?"

"Nothing."

Consternation. "Bint?"

"Later. After." Morrison pointed. "Sun come high then eat. Drink."

Perplexity. "No more?"

"No more. You good man here. I want you have much pig."

"Much tank," Bawi said. He discussed this with the others, who muttered in disbelief.

Dulani spoke.

Bawi said to Morrison, "Dis place," with a sweep of his arm, "you place."

Morrison bowed. "Much tank. Tank Dulani. Tank all man here."

Which Bawi did. Dulani seemed to fall asleep then, and the men dispersed. Bawi slipped the machete through his loincloth, where it hung awkwardly; he tried a few steps and removed it, brandished it, swiped once at an imaginary victim, and grinned at Morrison. After that he carried it in his hand wherever they went. It lent weight and menace to his gestures, and exaggerated his strut.

They toured the village again. Old women sat before

huts, wooden bowls in their laps, and ground flour with
large stones. "Cassawa," Bawi said. The women were
skinny and bent, save one, grotesquely fat, who could
barely reach her bowl. Some younger women, and many
children, followed them about until Bawi sent them
scampering off.

"Show me cassava," Morrison said, and Bawi led
him downstream, beyond the huts, to a grove of leafy
shrubs about as tall as a man, planted in regular rows.
In the dirt at the edge of the grove was something Morrison had never seen: a wooden hoe, all wood, and
hacked from one bough.

"You put this here," Morrison said. "The cassava."

"Yis sor. Ol' pop come, he bring cassawa. He put
here. More pop put more. Much cassawa."

"Ol' pop, what his name?"

"Name?"

"You call him what?"

"Yis, yis, name. Name Bawi. Name Tami. Bawi know
name. Ol' pop no name."

"No name?"

"Bawi not *know* name."

Another surprise. Morrison had wanted a beautiful
legend, sung down in poetry. Hiawatha. Then fled the
capital our pop with many wives, and led them here
and founded this our tribe. And so on. Bearing cassava.

Bawi showed him the roots. "Like dis no eat," he said
gravely. "Vairy fuckin bad," and he clutched at his
throat and rolled his eyes.

"How you eat cassava?" They strolled back toward

the huts. Children splashed and shouted in the stream, and fell silent to stare.

"Knife knife," and he made chopping motions, "like dis," and he pointed to the old women, "much sun. Much day sun." Ten fingers. "Much day go, eat cassawa."

Morrison could see the last little hut, shadowed and alone. "Kinjo," he said, wondering: Christian? Kinjo. Kinjo.

But this time Bawi only grunted, and quickened his step. Morrison peered. Someone lay motionless at the center of the hut.

"Bawi. Who's in the kinjo hut?"

"Mmm." They walked on while Bawi considered. "Bad man," he said. "Man do bad."

"What he do?"

Bawi hesitated. "No. No talk." He shrugged, and Morrison wondered if all men everywhere shrugged. "Man do bad, man talk kinjo t'ree day, no eat, man come back." He glared then. "No talk."

So Morrison shut up and followed him, but before they reached Dulani's hut, which Morrison knew now was the town hall, they were brought up short by a great racket in the forest, and dogs yelping. Men called out, and Bawi favored Morrison with his broadest grin. "You come," he crowed. They trotted. The whole village swarmed into the clearing and made for Dulani's hut. Morrison was jostled in the press and looked down to see that lovely girl at his elbow; she smiled shyly and slipped away. Now men came jogging out of the forest with their grinning, yapping dogs, and a shout went up: two of them bore a stout branch, and strung on the branch by his feet was a bloody animal. When they came closer, Morrison saw that it was a boar. He saw too that it was not strung, and he was pleased, and felt oddly at home, dis place my place, because it was what he had done with deer in Colorado. They had slit both hind legs low down, between bone and tendon, crossed the forelegs and jammed the forehoofs through the slits, and then broken the foreleg bones and twisted them across the slits. Like cotter pins. To make a sling. Over a pole or like a pack on your back.

Someone had speared the boar from in front, through the breast, just below the neck: the hard way, taking the charge. The hero was a young fellow, who smeared himself with blood now and grinned at the girls. Dulani congratulated him with a pontifical gesture. Then Malani the artist came forward, dipped a finger in the blood, and drew a circle on the young man's forehead, and everyone cheered. The hunting party laughed and strutted, and Dulani gave commands, at which there was more cheering, and some of the women ran off to obey him. Dulani spoke once more and there was Bawi again, at Morrison's shoulder, saying, "You come here, good come here." Morrison was pleased to think that he brought luck. He was watching the victorious hunter, who pranced and cavorted. The young fellow darted to a fat, giggling girl and squeezed her buttocks; she went on giggling and the villagers roared approval, and when they saw that the young fellow was in more than

one state of tall excitement there was thunderous rejoicing. He grinned and capered, making sure that no
one overlooked this secondary achievement; he managed to favor half the women with some small evidence of his devotion. Morrison found himself titter-
ing, and then bellowing glee with the others.

Later they hung the pig to bleed, and the machetes
were brought forth and shown to the hunters, who expressed reverent joy. Bawi explained to Morrison—it
took some time—that the machetes were common prop-
erty. One was now entrusted to the young hunter. They
were to be borne by heroes, but used for the village in
whatever way Dulani decreed. They would be inaugu-
rated tonight, in butchering the boar. Bawi asked politely if Morrison would honor them by staying to
dinner. Morrison regretted; previous commitments. Another time, perhaps. Bawi was sorry. But soon it would
be time for luncheon, and Dulani had commanded a
surprise. Morrison was delighted and flattered. Well,
Bawi admitted, the surprise was not altogether for Morrison, though he deserved one; it was in honor of the
boar. Morrison assured Bawi that he was flattered merely
to be invited. All that in grunts and groans and stone-age
English.

Morrison chewed at his gummy manioc and ignored
the women. He had awaited his servant girl with the
clammy joy of the failed sensualist, but she disappointed
him, yielding place to a withered, if flirtatious, crone.
Dulani groped and belched, and was fanned. Bawi ate

with zest. Soon a chant arose, and Morrison turned to see a line of women dancing forward, bearing huge gourds. The men approved loudly. Smaller gourds were dipped and distributed. Dulani spoke, and poured a few drops on the ground, and the men drank, Morrison too, delighted by the ceremony. Surprise.

It was a surprise, all right. Half blind, breathing fire from both nostrils, he set his gourd in the dust with exaggerated precision, allowed himself one roaring bawl of protest, and choked out, "Bawi. What is this drink? Petrol?"

"Dis good drink," Bawi said. "Dis . . ." and his eyes narrowed as he searched the past, "dis . . . *booze.*"

"Dis poison," Morrison said. "How you make dis booze?"

"Cassawa."

"You like this booze?"

"Oh yis sor," and that grin of love. "You like?"

"Oh yes," Morrison said. "Lovely. Full-bodied, slightly fruity. A trifle young."

"You say?"

"Nothing. Very good booze." He sipped again, and smiled, and ducked his head in thanks to Dulani.

In simple courtesy, and with burgeoning enthusiasm, he drank three gourdfuls. When Bawi suggested then that they go wawda, Morrison said woozily, "Yis sor. Go wawda. Sink like stone."

The sun belabored him, but dust sparkled and green water beckoned. Blue at dawn, green at noon. Odd.

Blinking and sniffing, he sauntered with the men. At the riverbank he removed his cap, sandals, and shorts, and a pleased cry went up.

"Oh yes," he said breezily.

"Ol' Tami not," Bawi said.

"Ol' Tommy boy," Morrison said. "Dis tommy man."

Bawi translated, and grunts received Morrison into fellowship. Gratefully he immersed himself; briefly he thrashed. He found a comfortable lodgment near the bank, and leaned back, and when he was sure he would not go under, he closed his eyes against the sun. Women's voices roused him, and the water's caress was suddenly unbearable; he was glad, for obscure reasons, that the women were downstream.

He slept.

Bawi woke him gently by placing a wet hand on his hot check, and Morrison smiled without moving, utterly renewed, brown, hard, cool, and—and unencumbered. Alone and yet not alone. Amphibian, straining ashore. Rising, he seemed to move in a new way, as if he were part vegetable, part animal, part river, part sun. With the men he strolled the bank barefoot, loose and strong, feeling the strength like a fever in his thighs and shoulders. The women joined them, and he accepted their curiosity, and returned it openly with one devastating pang, one excruciating, stabbing wish for the miracle, here, now and in sunlight; and then with a resigned and amiable equanimity. The men and women milled and chatted; Morrison stretched and lazed.

When he was dry he dressed, and when he was dressed
he felt foolish and alien.

"I must go now," he said.

Bawi nodded. "You come Dulani."

They walked slowly, in silence, to Dulani's hut. The
villagers no longer followed; perhaps Morrison had
ceased to be a novelty. They were alone with Dulani
and his women; Morrison saw the young, pretty one,
and they smiled.

Dulani spoke, sitting cross-legged as always.

"You good Tami," Bawi said. "You—" and he
paused, and searched his mind.

"Friend?" Morrison offered the word shyly.

Bawi nodded. "Friend. Bring good knife. We give
much tank. We give dis."

Dulani leaned forward, and presented Morrison with
a purplish stone of many facets, polished smooth, and
Morrison recognized a garnet. It was perhaps an inch
across and worthless. He accepted it with respectful gravity, examined it, and spoke in tones of awed approval.
Dulani was pleased.

"Dulani say, bridge bring you dis place, bridge good."

"You say much tank."

"Dulani say you come much. Come soon."

"Seven days. Maybe two seven days. I will come."

And again Dulani lapsed, shrinking back to a wake-
ful doze. Morrison checked a frown, a glance of concern. He smiled again at the girl and went away with
Bawi.

He saw much more now: snakelike plants wriggling toward gray-white blossoms; sprigs of green that might be grass and might be fronds; slender trees stripped of their bark; a column of black ants; the flicker of a red bird; the stippled fall of thwarted sunlight in a grove. In clearings yellow grass stood like wheat, with narrow trails—rats? mongoose? dwarf deer?—like streets and alleys, and the sun lay heavy, and he sweated. The flowers grew straight, and the blossoms looked upward, with no south to turn to. He saw red earth and red rock, screens of distant green. Carrion crows patrolled. Only the large animals never appeared. He no longer missed them. He would have enjoyed the sight of a live boar, but the mountain lions were a menace now and not a spectacle for tourists. Peace was valuable.

"Bridge soon?" Bawi asked.

"How much days?"

"How much days."

He counted off sixty.

"Rain come," Bawi said.

"When? How much days?"

Seventy. Maybe eighty.

"Much rain?"

"Oooh," Bawi said. "Much much rain."

At the gorge Morrison remembered. "Bawi."

"Yis sor."

"Big boom here," and Morrison's gesture exploded for him, "two, three days, not bad. Maybe much big boom. Not bad. Tommy make bridge."

Bawi grinned. "Oooh. Big boom."

"Boom boom," Morrison said.

"Boom boom boom." Bawi laughed in delight and spoke rapidly to the sentry, who also laughed. To Morrison they seemed to dance and shimmer in the sunlight, and he wondered suddenly why the colors were so stark: bright reds, searing yellows, shouting greens. The sun? Himself? A reversion to some forgotten meadow of childhood? Where everything is funny or sad, red or blue, rainy or sunny, friend or foe, chore or choice. He was like that, he knew: a thing was good, or a thing was bad.

"What's his name?"

"Galani."

Morrison said, "Tommy," and they nodded formally. "Bawi: all man name say 'lani.' What is lani? Dulani, Malani, Galani."

Bawi said, "Lani, all man like me." He gestured back toward the village. "All in dis man much hut, Lani."

"The name for the whole people."

Bawi liked that. "Peep. Peep name Lani."

"Bawi's name no Lani."

Bawi laughed now. "Bawi name Bawilani."

"Ah. Okay. I go now."

"Okay."

"Okay," the sentry said in a cavernous bass. They all laughed.

Morrison crossed lazily, and turned on the far lip to wave.

"You come soon," Bawi called. Galani was releasing the guide vine.

"I come soon," Morrison said.

Philips had returned with a compressor truck and diamond drills. "All in good order," he said. "Plenty of bits and so forth."

"Good," Morrison said "Tomorrow."

"Tomorrow." Philips smiled.

9

For the next two months there was no Morrison. There was only a brownish creature, doubtless vertebrate, something of the primate certainly and more than a little of the lizard. Large it was, and strong for its size, and it stood in the sun shifting its weight from buttock to buttock, relishing the play of heat on its shoulders and forearms. Now and then a phrase of music crossed its mind, and it smiled sleepily. The annihilation of Bernard Morrison had occurred suddenly but was not unwelcome: without resentment he became superfluous. Philips had accomplished that almost inadvertently. Philips was everywhere—instructing, exhorting, pleading, interpreting, hammering, tugging, sighting his sacred transit. It was consequently unnecessary for Morrison to be anywhere. He inspected, measured, verified, approved; and might just as well not have troubled himself. Philips seemed to grow taller and leaner, Morrison shorter and stouter. Eminent ectomorph announces conversion. Oh, he made an effort. He set the first charges himself, and lit the fuses, and later tried to relieve Tall Boy on the crane but was driven off by a doleful pout. "Never mind," he said apologetically, and went to sit under a tree and watch, like a boy with an ant farm.

They were in Tall Boy's hands. Morrison had been his first passenger, riding high across the gorge in an improvised sling, debarking on the south rim and marking spots for the diamond drills. The drillers rode across later on a wooden platform, trailing cables, and Morrison followed, still later, with dynamite. He lit a long fuse and repaired to his sling, and Tall Boy reeled him in, and trundled the crane to safety, and the men took cover, and in time there came a great roar, earth- and soul-shattering, echoing off a dozen slopes, dying with a hollow, rumbling, syncopated coda as tons of rock thundered into the gorge. "Very satisfactory," Philips murmured. Dust billowed like ground fog. Morrison wondered what Bawi was thinking. Then he blew the near lip, and where there had been two sheer walls there were two deep, roomy hollows, like recessed thrones from which two stony, hostile gods might glower; and when those had been leveled and cleared, the bridge was begun.

From the hollows grew a tangle of scaffolding, and on that scaffolding grew a strong, graceful arch of wooden forms. Jacob thought that the forms were the bridge, and they all laughed, and Philips explained: they were called falsework, and when they had met at the center, concrete would be poured into them, and when the concrete had set, which would take many days in this heat, that would be the bottom of the bridge.

Then they would bolt supports in place and throw
a road across. What road? Jacob asked, and Philips
pointed to the slabs that Serpa's men had brought: those,
he said, and eight more like them still to come, and he
explained that concrete could be poured and set anywhere and then moved, placed in position and bolted
just like planks. Jacob nodded wisely. It was apparent
that he would soon be explaining this to others. Ramesh cuffed him affectionately.

There were forty of them, and they drove up every
morning on trucks, hoods, running-boards, and went
back to camp at noon and into the stream like lem-
mings. The north rim of the gorge was a depot, a bus-
tling park of trucks, piles of rock, stacks of lumber,
pyramids of bagged cement, mazes of steel wire and
electric cable, barrels of nails and heavy bolts, cases of
tools and blades and spare bits, nests of canvas, coils of
rope, drums of oil, mounds of sand. Dust rose everywhere, pink dust off tires, white dust off stone and cement, yellow-gray dust where the jackhammers bored,
sawdust from the power saws. And the men swam in
heat. The pestilential sun drew endless scorching ripples
off overworked motors; the jackhammers at noon were
too hot to touch. Men snarled and choked and sweated,
and the dust matted on their sweat. The noise was constant: hammers bucking and stuttering, saws singing,
compressors drumming, engines barking and whining,
rock rattling and the earth itself growling. The Land-
Rover buzzed in and out like a hornet. The men sweated
through skins of dust and took the name of God in many

tongues. Faces cracked and peeled, eyes reddened, throats closed, skins gleamed. Long lines of sullen men besieged the tank-truck. A heap of hard hats lay unworn. "No one can blame them," Philips said. "It is too damned hot, and the hats are heavy." So Morrison tossed his own on the heap, and reverted to the jockey cap. Eminent haberdasher assumes purple.

What matter? He was not really working. He sat in the shade and admired Philips, who instructed carpenters, wire lathers, Tall Boy and the oilers. Even Ramesh, and naturally Jacob, went to Philips for orders. Between Philips and Tall Boy a new language sprang up, all verbs, yet all gestures. Without Tall Boy and his toy there was no bridge. Until the arch was completed, the carpenters worked from a platform, and the platform hung from Tall Boy's boom. Tall Boy sat higher than any man, grim and omnipotent, and rarely smiled before sunset. Is there a God? There is now. It weighs fifty tons and Tall Boy is its prophet.

Then in momentary disquiet Morrison busied himself. He stood with the men who were screening stones. Shake and rattle: abrasive dust. He played briefly in the sandpiles. He read labels on bags of cement. He went to Philips and grumbled. "Hey boss. You got work for me?"

"Grab a broom," Philips said. They contemplated the growing wooden arch, carpenters clinging and hammering, the sun fierce, the mystery of the gorge dwindling, defeated. "It will do," Philips said. "They really care, have you noticed that?"

"Yes. So do I. So do you."

"Oh yes. We will need more burlap. We should pour next week."

"You want me to go get it?"

"No. We can pick it up on the weekend."

"All right. It would only break up my day. Anyway I just dropped by to say hello."

Philips smiled demurely. "Nice to see you again."

"Yes," Morrison said. "Isn't it. Good luck with your bridge."

"Thank you," Philips said. "Were you planning to be here long?"

"Just passing through," Morrison said politely. "Good day."

Ramesh drooped, sighed, fanned himself. "Damn and blahst. I am played out. I have worked too hard. To the detriment of my serenity and detachment." It was Friday night, and even Philips sat subdued.

"Get another man."

Ramesh brightened: "Truly? But where?"

"One of the men will have a brother or a son," Philips said. "Ask them tonight. You will have a man by Monday."

"I will, I will. How simple. But the expense." Moths embraced his lamp. Philips was smoking a rare cigarette; smoke rose like a string in the still night.

"Hang the expense," Morrison said. "Devoe, Sims and Wheeler looks after its own. What would it be? Ten dollars a week? You know, something has happened to my tongue. The beer is marvelous. Everything I taste is rich and spicy."

"It is the gourmet food," Ramesh said primly.

"It is the hard work," Philips said. "Sitting about all day."

"Don't make fun of me." Morrison yawned. "I'm the last representative of a dying imperialism. We've saved a lot of money on the bridge. Left-over stone and local products."

"Cheap labor," Philips said.

"Cheap labor," Morrison agreed. "Underpaid engineers. We can afford an extra bus boy. If Philips would give up women we could afford two."

"Crazy man! Give up women," Philips said. "Come and get drunk tomorrow night. Use up some of that excess energy."

"All right. Try anything once."

"I will stop here," Ramesh said. "I am very tired."

"I think Moe should be your bus boy," Philips said. "It would solve all the problems in one stroke."

"Can't do that," Morrison said promptly. "Lose face with the natives. Open the floodgates. Revolution."

"Natives," Philips said in disgust. "You are a bloody wog yourself. All brown and half dressed and lying about while decent people work."

"A wog." Morrison was delighted. "Marvelous. Then I am part of the revolution of rising expectations."

"The next step is wog bint," Philips jeered.

"What?" Morrison sat straighter. "Bint. Tell me about that. What is bint?"

"You do not know?"

"No."

"What do they teach you—"

"You said that before. What is it?"

"It is British soldiers' slang for native women. Not very complimentary, by the way."

Morrison lay on the hard earth and laughed. Stars spun above him; he howled.

"What is so funny?"

"Nothing," he gasped. "Nothing. You can beat it out of me after the revolution."

"It is nice to see you," Martha said warmly as they shook hands in the soft light of late afternoon.

"It's nice to be back."

"Try not to bust up my steady customers."

"I am the most peaceful of men." Morrison smiled. "Let's sit down. Will you take a drink?" Almost he had said tek ah dreenk.

"No. But I will have coffee with you." She led him to a table. "It is early in the day for drinking. Where did Philips run off to?"

"Burlap. He went to town to pick up some burlap."

She gestured to Emanuel. "What will you have, and what is the use of burlap?"

"Coffee," he said, and she said, "Two," and Emanuel went away, and then Morrison said, "Concrete must not be allowed to dry too quickly. In heat like this above all. It is made of stones and sand and cement and water, with steel rods inside, and if it dries too quickly it shrinks away from the stones and steel and becomes brittle and weak. So after we pour it we cover it with burlap, and we keep the burlap wet for several days. We also use chemicals in the concrete to slow the drying."

"My, my," she said.

"Yes. Very complicated. That the success of a fine bridge should depend on burlap. And how is business?"

"Steady," she said.

"It will be unsteady tonight," he said.

They laughed together like friends, and Emanuel came with coffee.

"You are not the same," she said. "You are younger. There is something new inside you. Tell me what has happened."

"I can't," he said after a moment. "I really can't. I don't know. But in the last little while I've been telling myself that I don't want to go back. When I came here I thought I might die here, an accident, disease, whatever, and I remember wondering if I'd ever get back. Now I don't want to. It's like starting again. As if all the old sins were canceled."

"But that is not how you start again," she said. "You start again from inside, and not by going to a new place. Though it is not for me to say."

"You may be wrong. In French they say a new place changes the ideas. But you may be right, too, because you are a nice old Martha, with a good head on you," he said, and then, "there: you see? That's the kind of thing I wouldn't have said three months ago. Couldn't have. But I like telling you now."

"And why not? So you are different. And where are you going?"

"I don't know," he said. "I really don't know. But getting there is half the fun, as they say."

"Fun," she said. "If it is real it will not be fun always. Sooner or later you arrive, and sometimes it is not the place you set out for."

Which subdued him momentarily, but did not avert a long and happy night of rum, lies, and music. Not to mention an impromptu beauty contest at about three, won by Lollie with Morrison a close second.

Time itself altered. Days were measured in false-work, in steel rods anchored like bones, in the clank and belch of concrete mixers. Time seemed to drown in the timeless forest and eternal sun; seemed to replace distance as a measure, so that Morrison was not so many miles from Devoe, or from New York or Colorado or the war, but so many sunrises, so much carpentry, so many friends, so much concrete, so many desires, so much ful-fillment. And time moved only the one way: no round trips. Every morning meal, every eddy of dust, every carrion crow and every lion fly and every hairy spider, every half ton of concrete and every bottle of rum or beer, every grin from Bawi and every snarl from Phil-ips, all took him beyond recall and beyond appeal. Those were frontiers that closed behind the traveler. Not with a clang like gates, but with a rustle like grass.

He crossed another of those frontiers on a morning in August, when Tall Boy poured the last section, the hinge, the center. Tall Boy scooped up half a ton of wet concrete and dropped it like whipped cream. Again. And again. The fourth time Morrison called to him. "I'm going up. Let me get aboard."

"The cables may be hot," Philips said.

"I want to see it from above."

Tall Boy dangled the bucket; Morrison stepped out onto it. The cables were only warm. Then he was rising into the sunlight, with no signal, Tall Boy obliging. The men stopped work to watch, and shaded their eyes. He saw the bridge as he would never see it again; as in his drawings, yet not his own. It lay sprawled beneath him, almost ugly with the forms still in place; but it was a bright white, and its line was an austere melody, and it was all of Bernard Morrison that would survive. He knew that there would never again be one like this, as there was never again a first love.

The bucket hovered; it opened suddenly, vomiting wet concrete. Morrison drew the garnet quickly from his pocket, kissed it for luck, and tossed it into the creamy flow. With a kind of prayer; but to whom, or for what, he could not have said. It flashed purple in the sunlight, and was drowned.

Morrison's arm dipped, and Tall Boy swung him out and down, down, below the level of the bridge, far below, into deep shade. His sweat dried; he was cold; the sky vanished. The walls of the gorge were moist; below him black rocks stood blacker and sharper, black water boomed white. He saw a stranded plank, remembered a dropped hammer, and gave thanks that no man had been lost. The bridge of vines lay limp against the wall, clinging like a nest of vipers. Below, he saw no birds; heard only the boom and rush of the river.

From there his arch was ugly, only wooden forms and scaffolding. Far, far beyond, the sky again, and a solitary carrion crow.

He too was solitary now. The sun ennobled solitude; in this dank shadow solitude was a fearful loneliness. His hand was clammy on the cable, and melancholy nipped him like a moist breeze. He shivered, conscious once more of his flesh and its sad vulnerability; he dangled joyless. When he saw Philips peering down from the lip, he peered back, and their eyes locked for long seconds. Morrison felt rue, need, the desolate chill of exile; and pleaded silently that Philips lift the ban.

Philips raised a clenched fist, and Morrison rose.

They stood at sunset inspecting twenty meters of wet burlap. Sunsets were pure in the dry, cloudless air; at dawn the sky was shot with pinks and purples, but at dusk a bright orange penny settled into its slot, tugging night after it.

"Not bad," Philips said.

"I hope it dries white," Morrison said.

"It will."

After another moment Morrison said, "And no one killed or hurt."

"No. Not yet."

"Did you know," Morrison said slowly, "that in the old days when a bridge was finished the builders sacrificed a virgin and threw her into the stream?"

"No. That is fascinating."

"It is. To propitiate the spirits of the waters, who had been defeated and insulted."

"You are a fount of learning." Philips smiled. "Do you know that Tall Boy has asked me for a primer?"

Morrison laughed.

"Is that your doing?"

"Yes."

"Meddler. Missionary."

"Sometimes I think Tall Boy will inherit the earth," Morrison said.

"Do you mind that?"

"I'm all for it."

"You want Baptists in charge?" They laughed together.

"Why did you fall away?" Morrison asked him.

A crown of red sun fired the western jungle; the grasses smoldered. A six-o'clock bee shrilled close. Air lay cooler on Morrison's arms. He yawned peacefully.

"Little things," Philips said. "God was infinitely merciful and infinitely good, but just the same some of us would roast in Hell forever. That was like a broken promise. I do not break promises myself. But it was not any one thing. It was just the way I am. Barren ground for the seeds of the Lord. And you? Do you still believe?"

"I suppose not," Morrison said. "I don't think it matters. At the crucial moment God was never there.

Or it never seemed to make any difference whether he was or not. The innocent were tortured anyway. Girls were horsewhipped."

"Nobody really believes," Philips said. "If I really believed, I would sit in one place and pray, and neither eat nor drink until he took me. If I really believed, nothing else in the world would be of the slightest importance."

"If I really believed, I wouldn't be afraid of dying," Morrison said. "That would be nice."

"You fear death?"

"Don't you?"

Philips was silent, and then said, "I cannot tell. I do know that to be without God and still not fear death is the hardest thing. It is easy to be brave when a happy ending is assured."

Morrison looked again at the black face, and thought he saw wisdom. Then he thought it might be only bitterness, and mocked his own fancy; but Philips stood in placid repose, and resented nothing. Tired, perhaps dreamy. Morrison turned away, retreating from a rush of affection.

"The sun is gone," Philips said. "Come along."

Goray in a yellow shirt stumped the site like a gander, rocking from foot to foot as he marched briskly here and there. Serpa trailed behind him in a planter's hat, and bobbed at Goray's compliments. Morrison and Philips stood by in the grave solidarity of artists who must not laugh when dealers visit. Tall Boy, unemployed for the moment, inspected the official vehicle, a small air-conditioned sedan flying the national flag and emblazoned with seals, stickers, and departmental insignia. Its bored driver was masked by a newspaper.

"The disorder is astounding," Goray said, slapping white dust from his trousers, "but I must assume that you know your business. You are ahead of schedule."

"We are," Morrison said. "We have good men and the best of materials."

Serpa melted.

"How is the color?" Goray asked.

"So far so good. White as white."

Serpa swooned.

"And when can you unwrap it?"

"Another couple of days. Give us three weeks and you can drive across it."

"I should like that," Goray said. "I shall be the first."

Morrison and Philips did not correct him. On the arch stood Villem with a hose; the compressor thrummed, and rain hissed on burlap. The sun stood high, and Morrison was hungry.

"Let us walk across," Goray said. "I shall lead you into the promised land. Come, Serpa."

Serpa came; Morrison and Philips followed, and Tall Boy straggled after. Villem let them pass unsprinkled. Goray clambered out of the south abutment and trod Dulani's earth. He waddled downstream and looked across at the bridge of vines. "Ah yes. Ingenious. You might as well chop this away."

"No," Morrison said, louder than he had intended.

"Oh? And why not?" They all wanted to know. Philips bore a look of gentle, ironic wonder.

"As a favor to me," Morrison said weakly. "Suppose my bridge falls down?"

Serpa groaned. Goray cackled, and Tall Boy guffawed. Only Philips was silent.

"Leave it for a while," Morrison said. "It keeps me humble. Reminds me how much can be done with how little."

"Fair enough!" Goray patted his shoulder. "A good thought. A thought for the day. Pride before a fall, and all that."

"Native handicraft," Philips said.

Goray looked up sharply. "There are people back here?"

"Not that I know of," Philips said. "I was only spoofing."

"Oh. Good. Look at that." Goray flapped a hand to the west, to the long green slope, to the miles of forest and the distant hills. "I tell you. Some day we will be a rich country."

You are already a rich country, Morrison wanted to say, but he knew it was not true. He felt rich himself. Richer than Goray and almost as rich as Philips. "I'm hungry," he said. "Shall we go back?"

"Of course, of course," Goray bustled. "You have been working all these hours."

Philips caught his eye, and Morrison pinched away a possible smile. "It is very hot," Philips said to Goray. "You want to be careful after the air-conditioning."

"Yes. That is true. Well, well, follow me."

And he led them back out of the promised land. Morrison seemed to remember, but was not sure, that Moses had died within sight of the promised land but had never set foot upon it. The memory depressed him.

Food, however, heartened him, and the sight of Goray gobbling it down beside the stream was a small cabaret in itself. Ramesh served them, and Jacob scurried in awe. This wet-eyed Hindu and his fawn of a bus boy, Morrison thought: feeding forty men three times a day from the world's oldest steam calliope. The new bus boy was called Percival, and was banished to the service of lower orders; not for him, upstart, was this august assemblage. Morrison could not remember which of King Arthur's men had begun as a scullion, but did not think it was Percival. And in what chapel of silver and napery, he wondered, from what ambassadorial plate, is Devoe lunching on this sunny day? I must write him. Dear Sir: and what have I to say? I broke bread today with a politician and a Portagee. Something has been happening to me but I am not sure what. Everyone speaks kindly of you. I would like to be appointed emperor of our office here and you can have the refund on my ticket.

He set down his mess kit with one wild throb of his—well, of his soul—that brought tears to his eyes.

Why not? *That* has been happening to me. He listened to his own heartbeat.

"Excuse me," he said. He stepped to the river, almost

breathless, and stripped, and plunged. He lay on his back in the water, squinting against a sky that was all sun. Well. Dear God. What a silly idea.

They stood at the car, and Morrison was accepting more effusions when Ramesh called, and trotted to them. "Forgive me," Ramesh panted, and Morrison remembered that the man was over sixty. "Forgive me, but my radio has just told me that General Ros is once more in the Cabinet. I thought perhaps Mister Goray should know that before returning."

"He should indeed," Goray said pensively. "Oh ho. Oh ho. I thank you."

"What does it mean?" Morrison asked.

"Mean? Mean? Who but Ros can tell? The question is, how it can be used. Whither now. However" —a fat black forefinger waggled—"it means the government is safe. If the government were in real danger he would sit by, outside, and hope to pick up the pieces. If he is of it, he stands or falls with it. So." He rubbed his hands happily. "Good. Perhaps we can get some work done now. No more shooting in the streets."

"Has there been much?"

"Once a week an incident. The trouble is that we cannot predict them. It is disconcerting. On a Monday morning it is very discouraging. And diplomats hector us at cocktail time. Well, well, well."

"Then it was good news," Ramesh said. "How fine."

"A tick of the watch," Philips said. To Morrison his eyes said, What are all these Caesars beside a good bridge? Morrison smiled sadly.

"Then I must get back," Goray said. "I thank you for your hospitality."

"And I." Serpa bowed.

"Bring a brass band next time," Morrison said. "And a red ribbon to cut."

"By all means," Goray caroled. "And a photographer, and several pretty girls. Good-bye, gentlemen."

And good-bye it was, after the inevitable round-robin of handclasps. But Goray had another last word; he poked his head out the rear window, and sunlight flashed from his glasses, and he said, "Do you know, Philips, some days I have the distinct impression that we are becoming a country. Any day now we will be expropriating American firms," and he fizzed mischief at Morrison, and rolled up his window.

When the sedan was screened by its own dust, Morrison said, "Why go half way? Why not declare war on us?"

"That too," Philips said cheerfully. "But one thing at a time. Come on. A dip. I am tired of dignitaries."

"Dignitaries. Serpa?"

Philips laughed aloud, showing all his teeth, and Ramesh giggled. Morrison was immediately ashamed of himself.

Twice in September he went to the village, crossing his arch on a Sunday morning and proceeding alone over the hill, down that stunning yellow slope to the wall of trees, meeting Galani there. They have pulled back their sentries, he thought sadly; but he was sure that they had spied from the crest, and that stories were told before Dulani's hut. And that Bawi was aching from the effort to understand, to foresee. Bawi remained ebullient, always affable, clutching at new words, naming birds, shrubs, insects; presenting his Tami formally to more of his men and women. The women's names seemed to begin with vowels, and Morrison saw himself reading a monograph at a convention of pale anthropologists. That they eat slugs, gentlemen, must not be taken amiss. I notice escargots on today's menu. (Laughter.) Their rudimentary notions of marriage are evidence of sophistication; we are only now approaching their dispassionate flexibility, and I must tell you that my own marriages were rather rudimentary. (Laughter.) They share what they have. (Laughter.) They do not strike children. (Uproarious laughter.) They do not kill each other. (Unrestrained hilarity.) They have never fought a war, and have no word for nation. (Peal upon peal of convulsive merriment; the meeting stands adjourned.)

The girl who had served him was called Alalani, and served him again, and he understood—able to think now, and not merely to stare—why she had been absent that once. Plump and naked, she had blinded him, a primeval succubus; but when he greeted her, and she spoke, she became a woman, and he noticed a stray leaf clinging to her frizzy hair, a grain of sleep in her lashes, the goose-flesh of her nipples, a broken fingernail. He spoke to her with grave courtesy, and then Bawi led

him away, to teach him how to fish. They tramped far
upstream, and Bawi wove a basketlike net of green
withes, and impaled a rubbery slug on one withe, and
slung the net from the bank on two frail vines. Then
they lay waiting. They lay waiting for an hour, and Morrison expressed impatience. Bawi grinned his jack-o'-
lantern grin and said, "We go," and hauled in the net.
Morrison learned that it might take an hour to catch a
fish, or a day. They were big fish, flat, three to five
pounds he reckoned from Bawi's description. They were
called perai, and they had teeth. They would not bother
bathers in the absence of blood. At certain times women
were not permitted to bathe. Morrison never saw a perai
that day, but the fishing was restful. Later Bawi remembered that one of the men had lost two toes to a perai.

After his second visit that month he took Bawi to see
the bridge. "No more men dere?"

"No more. Only Bawi and Tommy." But Bawi approached the crest of the hogback with caution, and
reconnoitered before descending. The supports were up,
and part of the road in place; Morrison explained that
they would now place the rest of the road, and erect
railings, and then they would be finished and would go
away.

"Dis side go what place?"

"No road this side," Morrison said, uneasy at the un-
reasonable truth. "Maybe later."

"Road come by Lani?"

"Maybe. You want to go on the bridge? To the other
side?"

"No."

"No other man there."

"No." Bawi chopped aimlessly with his machete. Morrison saw that he was sulking.

"Listen, Bawi. On the other side, no more bad man. No more Tami, like me. All men there like Bawi. They won't hurt you."

" 'Urt?"

"Make bad. No more make bad. No more boss Tami." Morrison sweated; it had been a long, hot walk, and the sun was directly overhead. "Maybe later man like Bawi come to Lani. He bring good things. Knife. Medicine."

"Messin?"

"Man sick, medicine make him good."

Bawi shrugged.

Oh hell, Morrison thought. Maybe he's right. What do they need? Nothing. What will they get? Television.

The bridge was white and solid, comforting. "Bawi," he said, "it's all right. I tell you. It's all right."

Bawi frowned, and tried to grin, and said, "No. Vairy fuckin bad."

Morrison laughed, and said again. "No. Listen: I come again. Seven days. Talk more."

"Good. Tami come." He glanced up suddenly, and pointed, and said excitedly, "Look look!"

Morrison saw nothing: the hills to the east, the forest, the sky. "Look at what?"

"Rain come."

Morrison looked again, and saw a wisp of gray cloud

miles off, fragile and solitary. "Rain?" He laughed. "Not much rain."

"Rain come." Thirty fingers.

No bigger than a man's hand, Morrison thought.

Ramesh heard him with some wonder and more delight.

"Take this," Morrison said, "and buy five cases of rum, which will be a bottle for each man with some left over. When you pay them off, give them each a bottle with my thanks."

"My goodness," Ramesh said.

"Big spender." Morrison shrugged. "They did a hell of a job. Nobody was killed and the least we can do is spill some liquor to the gods."

From the approach it was not a bridge now but a road. The railings had still to be set in place. Otherwise there was no work for the specialists, so they had all been impressed into janitorial service. Trucks came in empty and went out full of left-over art and science. It was Philips's phrase: "Left-over art is garbage. So is left-over science. Like Lamarck. There is no use for it, so it is carted away. You think history is a museum, but you never see the garbage dump out behind."

"My dear colleague," Morrison said loftily, "history is not a museum. It is a delicatessen, and the people are pickles."

"Now what does that mean?"

"How the hell would I know? That's how you talk, not me."

"By God," Philips said, rather pleased. "You were having me on."

"Right. Can it be getting hotter?"

"No. There is moisture in the air."

"Ah, yes. Rain come."

An end and a beginning. One bridge. There would be more. He had said nothing of his hopes but had examined maps like a child on Christmas morning. So much to be done. Roads, bridges, dams. He was not sure how Philips would take it; and what Philips said would be important. He was almost shocked when he understood how important it would be. I must tell him at the right moment.

"Tall Boy has asked me for a Coleman lantern," Philips said.

"Inheriting the earth is hard work."

"Yes. So is changing it. It is hard to believe that we have finished here."

"You enjoyed it."

"More than anything I have ever done."

"Me too," Morrison said. "It felt important."

"It was. You could never count the people we have done something for."

Morrison only nodded, but he was moved.

That night Ramesh came to his hammock. "If you please, Mister Morrison."

"What is it?"

"It is Jacob. He would like—if you do not object—"

"Oh, come on. What is it?"

"Well, you see, he does not drink. And if you do not object—my, my. This is embarrassing. If you do not object, he would rather have the money. He is saving to marry, you see. His young lady will not marry him until he has a bicycle and a parasol for each of them." Ramesh smiled apologetically, and shrugged at such foolishness.

"A bicycle and a parasol," Morrison murmured. "Yes. Of course. Tell him yes."

My God, my God! I love this country.

10

He went back to the village on a Saturday, crossing his own bridge and hiking happily along the familiar trail, sniffing in curiosity at a thick yellow sky. It was not Galani but another who greeted him silently at the edge of the forest and permitted him to pass, gesturing broadly with the machete. Morrison bore strange cargo: an empty rum bottle, ten gas lighters guaranteed at a hundred lights each, and fifty barbed fish-hooks with two hundred yards of nylon line.

Bawi once more said oooh and aaah, and this time the whole village came to see, thronging the dust before Dulani's hut. Morrison smiled at Alalani, at Malani, at all of them. He asked Bawi to convey his hope that these things, too, would be shared. "Oh yis sor," Bawi said. Morrison explained the lighters, but had no need to explain the fish-hooks, two of which were given immediately to boys. Bawi himself cut a few feet of line for each of them. Morrison taught him a fisherman's knot; Bawi in turn taught the boys, who rehearsed it twice, gravely, before dashing to the river. And when Dulani had spoken, and Bawi had said much tank, all man much

tank, Morrison said, "This come cross bridge," and Bawi
was thoughtful.

The village returned to work, and Dulani to his doze.
Morrison knew by now that the chief was sick, deficient
—blood? nervous system? The sight, or the thought,
of blood and disease no longer roused loathing in Morrison, that too had receded, but Dulani was something
else—a mystery that inspired not the diagnostic impulse
but a prickly horror: the unknown, the hand of God.
There was sharpness to a wound, finality in death; in
Dulani there was only disease.

Morrison moved off, following Bawi in an aimless
ramble through the village. With the machete Bawi
pointed to a dog, brown, smooth-coated, blunt-muzzled,
tongue lolling: "Dis one good. Much pig."

Morrison was indifferent to dogs. "Bawi: you have
big cats here?"

"Cats?"

"Mountain lion. Jaguar."

"No, no," Bawi said. "One time, hagwa. Long time
back one hagwa. No come now."

Can't have everything, Morrison thought. Cross it off
the list. Distinguished visitor like me, too; not one cat.
Eminent—eminent—but he had forgotten the fancy
word for cat-lover. Voices disappointment. Registers protest. The women were grinding cassava, and Alalani
was among them, sitting awkwardly in the dust like a
shiny leather doll, her legs wide and the wooden bowl
between them tight against her belly, her round young

breasts bobbing and swaying as she drove the stone
pestle in its circular path. An older woman spoke; Alalani giggled. She was glossy, not a wrinkle. Near her
drab birds like sparrows pecked at spillings. The glare of
the day had diminished, the light was coarser; above
him clouds strayed like lost sheep, and carrion crows
flapped listlessly. Morrison too was listless; it was the
shift of wind, the change of weather, that had driven
him across the bridge a day early. Two little girls played
a game with pebbles, squatting and intent; they did not
smile as he passed.

"Rain come," Bawi said.

"Last time you said thirty days," Morrison chaffed.

Bawi caught his tone and grinned. "Come soon.
Come soon."

"Bawi: what does Lani mean?"

Bawi blinked. "Name all peep. Lani."

"I know. But does it mean more than that? La means
water. Are the Lani the people of the water?"

"Ah, ah! Yis sor!" Bawi clapped his hands in glee.
"Long long time Lani place by wawda. By big wawda.
Lani come here, come much day." His hands said a hun-
dred days.

"That many days to come here from the water."

"Yis sor."

They must once have been good fishermen, Morrison
thought; and they have forgotten even that. "What is
kinjo?"

Bawi was shocked. "*You* kinjo man."

"White man?"

Now he was perplexed. "Yis sor. Whi' man. Big whi'
man, kinjo. Big big whi' man."

"I don't understand. You mean a tall man?" With
his hand he explained.

"No no. Dis place Dulani big man. Whi' man Dulani, kinjo."

"I don't understand."

They walked together, Bawi's head bowed. The sun
was lower; Morrison had never seen the village softened
by evening shadow. He felt almost cool.

"You come," Bawi said. "Come Dulani."

Dulani saw no bar to Bawi's wish, but called certain
elders to him. Bawi orated. Morrison understood nothing; only that Bawi sought a boon. The elders sat before
Dulani in a semicircle, and murmured when Bawi
paused. They wore loincloths and seemed rather sleepy,
as though the call to duty had come at nap-time. One
scratched himself incessantly. One glanced at the sky
and grimaced. One was Malani, who beamed at Morrison.

"Bawi tell, you good man, you bring knife, you bring
good ting, you . . . friend. Bawi tell, you come look
kinjo. Dis man," and he waved at the six elders, "say yis,
say no."

They said yis. Dulani rose, with difficulty but without help. He nodded slowly, seemed to forget why he
had risen, and hobbled feebly to a corner of his hut. He
unfolded what looked like a lap robe—a boar's hide,

Morrison guessed—and withdrew a cloth bag. He returned to his seat and Morrison saw that the bag was a simple cotton bag with a drawstring. He had once owned such a bag, and the memory of it was suddenly sharp. A rabbit's foot, a flawed marble . . . thirty-five years. It had been a nuts-and-bolts bag and bore the name of a hardware store. He could smell the coarse cloth and the stain of oil.

The elders murmured again. In the manner of a myopic tailor Dulani loosed the drawstring and peered within. With finicking delicacy he inserted thumb and forefinger.

He withdrew a silver coin, and offered it to Morrison. Morrison leaned forward respectfully and accepted the coin with care and elegance.

They watched him in silence.

The coin was a shilling. The words stood bright, one shilling, and the date, 1940, and ringing the head this legend: GEORGIUS VI D:G:BR:OMN:REX. F͞D. I͞N͞D, J͞M͞P.

King George.

"Ah," he cried reverently. "Kinjo!"

Murmurs, smiles, a gracious, graceful, gratified turn of Bawi's wrist, like some dandy Louis with a perfumed kerchief.

Dulani's hand, supplicant and steady, awaited the coin; he bowed, owlish, restored the shilling to its reliquary, and dismissed his court.

Amid outcries and laughter the two boys paraded their perai; villagers chanted and clapped, and Bawi grinned his grin and rubbed their heads like any man. "Plenny eat," he said. "Tami eat."

"Yes. Thank you." Morrison wondered: raw? No. Baked, in a ritual complexity of embers, the fish wrapped in broad leaves. The cooking was performed by one of the elders, and another delivered the benediction, an incantation, while Dulani rocked and swayed. Morrison asked Bawi what the man had said.

"He say, want much fish."

"Did he give thanks?"

Bawi nodded. "Much tank big fish."

"Thanks to who?"

"No no. No tank man. Tank big fish. All fish pop."

He had thanked the father of all fish. That was reasonable. Send us more fat sons. The smell of the baking fish roused hunger in Morrison, fishy and woody at once. "Will we drink cassava booze?"

Bawi grinned.

The sun was low when they sat on the ground to eat. The perai was a flat monster, probably five pounds, eyeless now, and nine of them ate it: the six syndics and the boss and Bawi and Morrison. The booze was even stronger than Morrison had remembered, but all tastes were good now. He seemed to be thinking with his body and not his brain, using senses and not logic, feelings and not principles: what was, was. The fish filled the belly and the booze filled the head, and that was what mattered. Belches resounded, and small whoops of pleasure. Manioc patties went down like hot cakes, which come to think of it they were. Morrison offered compliments to the chef. His leaf was twice filled, his gourd never empty. Alalani served him; when she bent for his leaf, her breast caressed his arm, and his heart swelled, and he scrabbled for the gourd, needing a long swallow of corrective fire. He trembled. Long shadows purpled the dust, and beyond their circle the evening was still, only the cheerful call of a child and the murmuring breath of the village. As the sun set, Alalani returned and set mangoes before them, and Dulani made another short speech.

"Bawi," Morrison asked later, "when I go back, can you give me cassava booze in this?" He tapped the rum bottle.

"Ooh." Bawi was overwhelmed; joy suffused him. "Vairy fuckin good. Yis sor." Morrison saw that he was happy to be able to give something, anything; and Morrison was touched.

The booze flowed endlessly. As the sun declined, so did Morrison, and with the last light he fell into a glazed, cheery stupor; he lay like a smile made flesh while the elders chatted and picked their teeth with fishbones.

"Dis man say bridge good," Bawi said. "Bridge good. Good ting come."

"My pleasure," Morrison breathed. "Engineer Morrison. My card."

Bawi contemplated him. "Tami sleep."

"Good." Morrison had drunk a pint of cassava booze, he guessed. "I find that I am unaccustomed to the vin du pays."

But Bawi was chatting with the others again. Then he spoke: "Tami sleep kinjo hut."

"Good." The sooner the better. "Fitting. Eminent snoozer shares royal digs."

"Tami talk much," Bawi said appreciatively.

His pillow was the ancient haversack: stiff canvas and greening grommets, with no name or number. The dirt floor was hard but there was no choice; he directed a short prayer to the god of venomous snakes and spiders. Get me out of this alive and I will endow a herpetarium to the glory of the Great Bushmaster. He fizzed and gurgled pleasantly. A night on the town. His town. The old home town. The parable of the prodigal and the fatted perai.

Bawi unfurled a length of Portagee cloth: sheets, no less. In the last hush of light all he could see of Bawi was the grin. Bawi touched his shoulder and melted into the night. Morrison stripped and lay on his back wondering if he would awaken black, or a small child. The disappearing engineer. International scandal.

The frogs were noisy. They spoke several languages. Kekekek. Reep-reep-reep. Kachung. Kachung. Reep. And were answered from the forest: insects? birds? Kaark. Kaark. Tututu. Eee-eee. Kachung.

A light: he sat up, his heart thudding. It was Bawi with a lighter, and behind him Alalani, with a gourd. Water. She set it down and stared at his body. He felt exotic again, and knew that she wanted to touch him; a dull flicker in his loins answered the dull flicker of flame. He drew a long breath, and his heart thudded wilder. Oh God: this is the wrong thing to pray for but oh God. Bawi backed out of the hut, and left him blind. He heard her breathe.

She touched him then, and he shuddered, and the dull flicker became a leaping fire. He wanted to cry; no use, no use; but there was no need. He touched a shoulder, a full, hanging breast, the sweet swell of a hip, and he rose to her answering caress like the first man.

The rest of that night was delirium.

And what a sunny morning! He awoke laughing, alone, alive with relief. He drank from the gourd, and rushed to the stream for a wash; the village was long awake. Women snickered as he trotted by, and he laughed at them, and back at the kinjo hut he found a mango on his bed. Bawi joined him there, that silly grin splitting his silly face, and Morrison laughed again, slobbering mango juice onto his chest. Cock-of-the-walk. He quickened all morning to titters and nudges, and remembered a morning in his seventeenth year: do I look different? does it show? Bernard Morrison: what have you done? You man about town, you rascal and rake, you gay old dog!

When he left they came to see him off. All but Alalani. A taboo? They laughed and whooped, shouted and murmured, and in the presence of so many he was at first embarrassed. But even Dulani came to the edge of the village, and even Dulani was laughing, and it was a fatherly Dulani who placed the bottle in his hands and cackled contentedly, eh-eh-eh. At that, Morrison simply let go, and bellowed laughter; so they all let go, and peals of jubilation sent him on his way.

11

It was October then, and the light lay heavier upon the land; shadows crawled softer, and insects chirruped softer, and at dawn there was a trace of dew. With the railings in place, with every plate and bolt true and tight, some of the men, those who had been hired to do just one kind of work, were sent away. Those who stayed were those who had built the road. Now instead of unloading they loaded, and trucks went in full and came out empty. Morrison did not favor the dumping of waste into the gorge; he warned the men, who grumbled but agreed. Small bits and pieces went over the edge all the same. Morrison only smiled.

With no more than a week's work left, Morrison gave the men an added day off, a Friday, and the four who had become friends were left at the bridge, among the dwindling piles of sand and stone, the few coils of wire, the two crates of dynamite, the few bags of cement, the small stacks of plates, the lonely barrels of nails and nuts and bolts. The lumber was long gone. The roadbed was bordered by broken rock and small craters of dusty, trodden grass, and late in the morning Morrison thought that he might be strolling on the moon, or through a bombed and deserted town. He and Philips had come up in the Land-Rover, leaving Ramesh and Tall Boy to laze and bathe and prepare a good meal. Philips drove, and Morrison sat slumped again with his knee banging on the useless protuberance. He would some day write to the manufacturers, but at the moment he enjoyed the rhythm of it. He was solid this morning, well rested, with life in his blood and bones and muscle. Ah, he felt fine! He smiled up at the carrion crows, who smiled down at him. His large hand was moist on the leather case of his small camera. He was sorry that his work was done, and this tag-end, the taking of photographs, was a sad task. He had taken photographs of the bridge in all its stages, like a botanist with a slow-blooming plant, and he had begun already to feel empty and lost.

But there would be another, he knew. And for a few moments he dreamed of the roads and bridges and buildings that he would give to this hot country where he had found another youth.

"That is handsome," Philips said. They had come out of the shade at the head of the straightaway, and the bridge from there was straight and pure, white and truthful.

"Yes. I wish we could do without railings. They spoil it."

"They do. But it is a bridge and not a painting."

Philips steered them off the road, and they bumped and lurched into a patch of shade. Morrison slipped the leather strap around his neck, and they walked to the bridge; the camera bumped warm against his hairy belly. He snapped shots from the level, on both sides, and from beneath, which he liked better: he scrambled down into the abutments, sat on the shadowed rock floor, and shot upward into the simple looming arch that was, for him, the bridge, and would never be seen by travelers. He took a few of Philips on the bridge, and Philips returned the favor. They walked downstream for half a mile, to where the lip of the gorge curved away and down and became a hillside. Walking back, Morrison paused to photograph the bridge of vines, hanging dead from the lip. He was not stirred by its death. It had served.

They crossed to the side of Bawi's people then, and climbed the dusty slopes of tall grass to the east. They climbed far, sweating and fighting off lion flies, threading a crooked path through the grass, and when they had come a mile they stepped onto a slope of speckled gray rock that leveled at its crest. There they sat, panting and running with sweat. Morrison dried his palms on his shorts.

They were high up. Looking to the north, they could see the glittering blue loops of their river, and the copse where Ramesh and Tall Boy were. To the west was their bridge, in profile far below them; and beyond the bridge, beyond the gorge, endless miles of green rolled relentlessly to the heart of the continent.

Morrison was silent and thoughtful. He was thinking, my heart is full; I know now what they mean when they say that.

His bridge gave form to the whole visible world. He thought of a silver bow in a woman's dark hair. The bridge was an arched band of white, and it pulled tight the chaos of jungle, the swaths of savanna, the blotches of bare gray rock. The landscape melted, and poured itself into his bridge, and was no longer rude, no longer free; it was man's now.

"You might look twice at it," Philips said quietly. Morrison wanted to touch his shoulder and say, "I am staying," but did not. Instead he said, "Yes," and raised the camera.

Then they sat for a while high above the world, minding the sodden air but unable to go. What would he remember when he had forgotten all the rest? Alalani? Or this moment, he and Philips alone with his bridge that would be Bernard Morrison for as long as—no, he thought. Someone will bomb it some day, and he was moved to a painful sadness because he knew there was every chance of that.

"Yes," Philips murmured. "I think later on it will be a great pleasure to say, 'Oh yes. That is my bridge.' "

"Your bridge."

"Yes. Of course it is more yours than anyone's. But you know how men are. When you are gone it will become mine."

And he almost told Philips then, but did not. He said, "Maybe once in a while you could say 'It was designed by a fellow named Morrison.' "

"It was designed by a fellow named Morrison. Yes. I could say that."

"Practice," Morrison said. "It will come easier after a while."

In one hand Ramesh held the lid of the great iron pot, and in the other a wooden spoon that he seemed to be kissing. The fire leapt, and steam drifted. "Ah," he said, and closed his eyes to smile. He heard Morrison and Philips then, and clapped the lid quickly onto the pot.

"What are you so proud of?" Philips asked.

"You are just in time," Ramesh said. "Go and wash and wait to be served. Tall Boy!"

From the river Tall Boy answered, a loud grunt.

"Put on your pants and come here and serve."

"Why I need pants?"

"This is a formal luncheon," Ramesh said sternly. "What is that you have, Mister Morrison?"

"Something for a formal luncheon," Morrison said. "Don't open it."

Ramesh saw the label. "Rum."

"Not any more," Morrison said. "Patience. A tick of the watch." He set the bottle in the dust, in the shade where they would eat, and he and Philips stepped into the river. "That's good," he said. "Oh that's good."

Tall Boy emerged streaming.

"The Loch Ness monster," Morrison said.

"Unwreathèd Triton," Philips said.

"Absolutely."

"What is in the bottle?"

"Mead," he said.

"Have you ever drunk mead?"

"No. You?"

"No. I wonder if it is still made."

"Not that I know. I don't even know what it is."

"Honey," Philips said. "They make it from honey."

"Well then this isn't mead," Morrison said.

In his shorts and red fez Tall Boy brought the mess kits. He stood grinning at their blank surprise. "And there is enough for twelve men," he said.

Morrison was awed. "This is poule-au-pot," he piped finally.

Ramesh had joined them. "If you wish. More humbly, I call it boiled chicken. With spices."

"Bravo," Philips said. "My compliments. My respects."

"And mine," Morrison said. "I don't know how this stuff will go with it, but give me the cups."

He poured, and handed out the cups. "To the bridge," he said. "To many more."

"Hear, hear," Ramesh said. Philips and Tall Boy made agreeable comment, and they drank.

"Lord Jesus," Tall Boy said, when he could, and sucked in air like a man drowning.

"A little something some friends gave me," Morrison said.

"Fine friends," Ramesh gasped, and shut his eyes tight. "Damn and blahst. My goodness."

"You do get about," Philips said. He was wiping his eyes with the back of his thick hand. "Do you know what this is?"

"Of course," Morrison said.

"Where did you get it?"

Morrison jerked his head toward the bridge.

"You had better eat," Ramesh said. "Fill your belly first with something solid. In any case someone else may have to do the dishes. I am not a very talented drinker."

"Throw them out," Morrison said. "This is the captain's dinner."

Philips did not meet his eye. In one hand Philips held the torso of a small chicken, and with his teeth he was stripping the flaky white meat from it. He spat a small bone. "The end," he said. "There is always a moment of sadness when a job is done."

"This booze make you happy again," Tall Boy said.

"There is only the one bottle," Morrison told them.

"Thank God," Ramesh said.

Morrison noticed for the first time—so late in the day!—that all the fragile, spindly treetops spiked straight up. He remembered parts of Colorado where they were all brushed eastward by the steady wind that blew down toward Kansas. Here they were bright black and green against the pale blue sky. He would keep an eye on them as he drank. When they blurred he would lie down. The climbing and the sun had made him sleepy.

"I'm going to stay on," he said suddenly, surprising even himself. "I'm going to ask them if I can stay on here and run the office."

Tall Boy cheered, and Ramesh bobbed his head in delight. But Morrison was watching Philips, who stared owlishly for a moment, and took another sip from his cup, and then said, unsmiling, "I am glad. I really am. But are you ready?"

"Ready? I—oh, hell. It isn't easy to tell a man that you love his country. Or maybe not the country, just *being* here." Morrison too went to his cup. This was, as he had said, not easy.

"Well, then, that is fine. The best of news."

"I thought you might—I mean, the table of organization."

"Oh no," Philips said, waving his cup in good cheer. "You are a good boss and I like working with you. You keep out of the way."

They all laughed. Morrison was still watching Philips, who winked now, and Morrison sat back, loose and happy. "There must be a lot to do."

"Oh, there is," Philips said, and shifted, lunging up off his elbow and sitting upright. "You amaze me. I hope you know us as well as you think you do. This is very good news." Morrison saw that he meant what he said.

"Well, thanks. I wasn't sure. But I want it," he said.

"More chicken," Ramesh said.

"Yes. And more booze. Cups, cups." A surge of elation made his head swim, and he checked the treetops because this was a hot day, and close, but they were sharp and clear against the radiance of noon.

Very good, he thought. Just drink now and keep your mouth shut.

Half an hour later Ramesh had performed a ceremonial dance, insisting that it was genuinely Indian, and Tall Boy had sung, reverberatingly, an obscene song, and Morrison, who had miscounted the now furry treetops, was lying flat on his back and rejoicing in his crew. He was feeling quite boyish, and had thought, at one point, that they were like a scrubby band of burlesque knights. There was Tall Boy of the Red Hat, and Ramesh of the Wet Eyes. And Philips of the Hard Nose. And Morrison of the Purple Helm. But he could feel pleasure on him like a new skin, and he was sure that his life had led to this. The flesh and blood of the war, and the flesh and blood of his marriage, and all the gray days before and between and after, stale days in one or another cheerless apartment; the mindless life that left him still hungry and thirsty and with no taste for tomorrow; the parties, smoke and gin and a sad, lonely, trapped woman backed into a corner with the hurt so plain behind her eyes that he would not add to it; and the better days too, hard, cold days edged with frost and the sunlight blue on the snow that his machines sullied; or warm days when the work went fast and well and his only sorrow was for the copper beeches he had annihilated; all those days had led to this, and it was not easy to quarrel with the past when you loved the present. And if he could call this place home!

"I hear something," Tall Boy said lazily.

"The voice of God," Philips said. "Or Lollie."

"The spirits of the river," Morrison said. "Looking for a virgin."

"You laugh," Tall Boy said. "But I hear something."

"So do I," Ramesh said sleepily.

They listened. Morrison heard the forest hum and snap, and the buzz of a locust.

Then he heard the clank of metal, to the north, and he sat up and groped for his cap. Philips too sat up, and then the others. Morrison blinked, and the day spun slowly; the sky was beaten gold, and floated. He tilted the bottle and let the last drops of liquor run into his throat, and he listened.

"By God," Philips said, and came to his feet like a cat, "it is our first customer. It is some sort of vehicle."

They knew he was right. All four of them scrambled up in excitement and ran, lurching only a bit, back through the grove and to the trailers at the roadside. The road was deserted, but beyond the curve they could hear the metallic rumble. They stepped onto the road and stood abreast, and now the heat came down like rain, and even Philips, who never seemed to mind heat, exhaled a sharp whuff of annoyance.

When they saw the first tank, Ramesh said, "Hey Rama," very softly, and no one else spoke until all eight had come around the bend and were bearing down on them in single file.

The officer was rangy and graceful, in his thirties, with tight-curled hair and an open, solid athlete's face. He stood taller than Morrison. In a small oblong above his breast pocket his name and quality were spelled out: MAJOR MACKENZIE. The high sun winked off his pips or crowns. He was for the moment hatless, and carried a swagger stick, and his short-sleeved shirt was perfectly unwrinkled. Above the other breast pocket were three campaign ribbons, and Morrison, giddy with booze and noonday sun, could not imagine what triumphs they represented. Good conduct, doubtless, and perhaps riot control and strike-breaking. Or rapine, buggery and genocide. But when the man spoke, Morrison was ashamed of his resentment.

"Good afternoon," said the major in a British voice. "You are the first people we have seen for many hours. I assume that we are near the new bridge."

Morrison turned to Philips, who answered, and Morrison was momentarily pleased with his own new delicacy, and thought, eminent diplomatist, but could not finish the thought.

"Yes," Philips said, and held forth a hand. "I am Philips, an engineer. This is Morrison. Our friends Ramesh and Tall Boy."

The major was bland and correct, and shook hands with all four. He introduced Captain Ten Eyck, who was stocky like Philips and wore glasses, and had a carbine slung on his shoulder. The tanks, behind them, radiated heat, and seemed to breathe heavily. In each turret stood a lieutenant: Morrison assumed they were lieutenants. The major reminded him of body-building courses advertised in cheap magazines, and he was ashamed of that resentment too.

"How far is the bridge?"

"About four miles," Philips said.

"Good. There is a stream near by, I believe."

"Through the woods, there. A quarter mile."

"Good. With your permission we will rest here for an hour or two."

Philips smiled. "Good of you to put it so politely. By all means."

"No objection if I station my tanks in the shade, there?"

"None. Have you food?"

"Yes, thank you. Are there other people here?"

"No."

"Nothing at all there to the west?"

"Nothing."

"Fine. Captain: tanks at five-yard intervals under those trees, facing west."

The captain said "Sir!" and walked back to give the orders.

"We were told that the bridge was finished," the major said.

"It is," Philips said. "We have a few days more of cleaning up." The tanks growled and clattered. Major Mackenzie invited the civilians to clear a way, and they all moved to the roadside. The tanks passed in a roar and Morrison marveled again at the size of them. In his war these would have been heavies but he supposed that they were now mediums. They flung up surprisingly little dust but stank of oil and hot metal. Morrison was sorry for the crews inside. He was sweating freely now, and not altogether from the heat of the day.

"No use to stand in the sun," the major said, and they

walked to the trailers under the trees. "We shall be here about two hours," he said. "Do you know the terrain on the other side of the bridge?"

Philips glanced at Morrison, who stood silent.

"What we could see," Philips said, "was scrub and small groves, and some grasslands. Beyond a mile or two I do not know."

"Thank you." The tanks had wheeled off the road and were crashing through the light underbrush. A small tree shivered down. The tanks roared and snorted, maneuvering. A flight of small yellow birds arrowed out of the forest and across the road, and disappeared to the west.

"What—" The word caught awkwardly in Morrison's tight throat, and he began again. "What are you planning to do over there?"

The major smiled and shrugged. "Take a look. Now: where is that river?"

An hour later Morrison was still sticky and sweating, but had a bad headache to distract him. He swallowed three aspirin tablets with a pint of water and sat cooling himself with the fringed fan. Ramesh and Tall Boy were at the river with the soldiers; he could hear the shouts and laughter of men at play. After a few minutes in the stagnant air, that settled on his skin like steam, he slouched to the refrigerator. He was half-way through a bottle of beer when Philips returned.

"That is the life," Philips said. "Thirty days off each year with pay. One of the lieutenants is a man I know.

I was drunk with him five years ago when he was a private, and he remembered. Small world."

"Quick promotion," Morrison said. "What are they going to do?"

"How would I know? That beer looks good. This heat is because of the moisture. Soon enough it will rain now." He plucked a bottle from the refrigerator and uncapped it, and stood, legs apart and feet splayed, back arched and mouth up, and drank off most of it. "Ah. Ah."

"They must have something in mind," Morrison said. His head throbbed. "Those are tanks."

"I noticed," Philips said. "I suppose they want to see if the Portagees are up to mischief. Or maybe just build an officers' club."

"There are people back there," Morrison said angrily.

"Oh, yes. So there are. Your bootleggers. Tell me about them." Philips lowered himself to the dust and sprawled back against the trailer.

"They're just people. Primitive. Good-looking and easygoing. Their ancestors hid back there to get away from the white man. They liked me. They were worried about the bridge and I told them it would be all right."

"You told them," Philips said.

"Yes. Tanks," Morrison said. "You don't ride around in tanks without a reason."

"Calm down," Philips said. "No government sends its people into unknown territory in tourist buses. Would it be more sensible to send Goray in a little red sports car?"

"Yes. What are they afraid of? God, they make me nervous!"

Philips shrugged. "You cannot argue with an army."

"That's what makes me nervous," Morrison said.

After a silence he said, "Oh, the hell with this. I'm going to see him. He must have orders of some kind."

Philips glared suddenly. "You and your bloody promises. You had no right to promise anything or even to stick your nose in there. Do you know how long it took us to free this country and make our own army? How many died doing it? Five years ago the major was probably a corporal in the white man's army, mopping latrines or serving drinks to the officers' wives. Leave them alone."

"No. At least he has to know that the people back there mean no harm. They're peaceful."

"He does not care. Believe me. Whatever his orders tell him, he will do."

"That's what I have to know," Morrison said. "I wish I didn't have this headache. I wish it was cooler."

"Go to your friends and warn them," Philips said. "Take the Land-Rover," and the bitterness in his voice bewildered Morrison. "Promises. Uncle Moe, schweitzering through the jungle, burning with second-hand indignation."

"Second-hand hell," Morrison said. "These people are my friends."

"Friends. Your wards, you mean. Uncle Moe's black orphanage."

"Shut up," Morrison said. "You don't know where you came from yourself. You could be one of them."

"Not bloody likely," Philips said tightly.

"I'm going to see the major."

"Good luck," Philips said, his eyes hard, his hand trembling. "Never say that to me again. Do you hear? Do you hear?"

Morrison put on a shirt. It was starchy under the arms and hung like a coat of mail. Because you could never tell with soldiers, he found his passport and slipped it into a breast pocket. Magic. Now he was protected and had marvelous powers. Perhaps he was invisible. Arrows would fall blunted from his chest. He was sick and sore as from too much brandy, and when he closed his eyes, walking down the shady trail, he almost lost the feel of up and down, and stopped for a deep, tremulous breath.

A picket halted him, which was almost laughable, but it seemed less and less like a day for laughing. "Morrison," he said. "The American. I want to see the major."

"Yes sir," said the man, and called to a corporal, who led Morrison to a patch of shade behind the cooking truck. The major and the captain and three lieutenants looked up at him with friendly curiosity, and the corporal went away. Morrison touched his purple cap.

"Mister Morrison," the major said. "Is something wrong?"

"I, ah, have a request," Morrison said.

"Please."

"It's about the other side of the gorge." He tried to address all of them, but his gaze came back to the major, who was sitting cross-legged like Dulani and holding a canteen in one hand.

"Go on."

"I'm a foreigner here and I have no right to ask favors. I know that."

"Please."

"All right. I was wondering if you could give me any clearer idea of your orders." He felt suddenly foolish and gangling.

But the major smiled pleasantly. "No," said the major. He sipped from the canteen but his eyes were steady on Morrison. Nothing bothers him, Morrison thought. Where is the swagger stick? He saw it then between the major's crossed feet, and he began to know, in a moment of light, how Indians had felt, Kenyans, Zulus, hunched in supplication before the bland, golden British colonel.

"I'm sorry to hear that," Morrison said sadly.

As if he had noticed the sadness, and cared, the major said, almost smiling, "If it was the old army I might rely upon your discretion. But we take ourselves quite seriously now. Live ammunition, and all. And then if it was the old army I would not be a major."

"All right," Morrison said.

"You have perhaps been a soldier yourself?"

"Yes. Once."

"Then," and the major spread his hands in fraternal good will. "The bridge is ready, and will hold?"

"The bridge is ready," Morrison said, "and will hold," and he moved to withdraw, but the major was speaking again.

"Mister Morrison. Why do you want to know about my orders?"

Morrison was silent, and looked at each of them for a tick. These are only men, he thought. Look: one wears glasses, and another is an Indian like Ramesh. And one is very black and one is light brown. And they are kind to children because they can afford kindness, and in the capital they drink when evening comes, just as I do.

"There are people back there," he said finally. "I told them no harm would come from the bridge."

"Well," the major said, "it was not an authorized statement."

"It was authorized by decency," he said.

The major sighed. "This is a border area, Mister Morrison. A most delicate border area. A confluence of governments and economies and ideologies and colors. You understand."

"I understand," Morrison said.

"What sort of people are these?" the major asked.

Morrison told him.

"Oh," the major said, already laughing, and then they were all laughing, quite relieved, dismissing him, "oh," the major said, "bush niggers. Hardly important, old man. Bush niggers," and they were all laughing.

"Their own people," Morrison said. "Their own people. You should have heard them."

He had gone back to Philips and for a long while had sat dumb in the folding chair with his hands clasped between his knees. His headache was gone—no, not gone, replaced; the heat seemed to be sucking his life from him. Soon he poured rum and water into a cup, and then again at a greedy gesture from Philips. While he sat numb, the soldiers drifted back to their tanks in twos and threes, and he watched them making small adjustments, grouping in crews and chattering playfully. The lieutenants checked their side arms with much clicking of metal, and chaffed their men. The major and his captain inspected and conferred. Ramesh and Tall Boy darted among the machines like children.

"Their own people," Philips mocked him. "Much they have in common, an army major and a bush nigger."

"They have a country in common, and a color. Not to mention a species. He'd cut them down without a second thought if he had orders."

"Sometimes you make me sick," Philips said. "No one is going to cut anyone down. And if he had to do it, there would be a reason. If we cannot open this country and make it safe, millions will die later and the rest will be slaves to—to you, with your computers and space ships."

"Sure," Morrison said. "How does it go? You can't scramble eggs without killing people."

"Oh, will you stop whining?" Philips flared. "All around us they die every day. Flies die and birds and monkeys and men. And are renewed and replaced.

Without reason. You too, and me, and soon. And you
see good and bad. Well, I see life and death, and life is
movement, and some movement kills other movement
as men kill lion flies. You cannot breathe without killing. Goray tried to tell you that. You have to accept that.
What is the matter with you suddenly?" Philips was
pleading, in anger. "For God's sake, man, stop this."

"I don't have to accept killing," Morrison said flatly.
"Or even uprooting. A shanty is a lot worse than a hut,"
and he stopped there because the major was approaching. The major walked with a perky swing to his hips
and shoulders. Ramesh and Tall Boy trotted along behind him. Morrison and Philips rose.

"I came to thank you both," the major said, "and to
tell you good-bye. Though we may stop in again on the
way back."

"By all means," Philips said.

Morrison said nothing, and tried to keep his face
empty. The major paused before him; there was more to
say. The major's dark eyes were wide-set and steady.
"You must forgive me, Mister Morrison, if I am
blunt." He rubbed his cheek with the round tip of the
swagger stick. Morrison saw nothing in his eyes: not
friendship, not enmity, not anger, not humor, not even
gravity. Only the steady expressionless look of the man.
"I was aware of your shock. But I deny your right to
judge. And I tell you further that it cannot matter to
you what is done here. All that matters is that *we* do it.
That is something you have never understood, you, ah,
foreigners. We do not require your permission and we

are indifferent to your approval. Or disapproval. And I do not mean to be inhospitable. History"—and he paused, gazed off into the distance and pursed his lips slightly, as if fearing the rebuke of some remote preceptor—"has withdrawn your mandate."

"I never had a mandate," Morrison snapped, "and never wanted one, and I am not here to preach but only to build, and I am tired of being mistaken for Cecil Rhodes. I only want to protect some friends that I seem to have made trouble for."

"Fair enough," the major said softly. "This is none of your business, but you almost make me wish that it were."

Morrison flung up his hands and turned away. He heard the major's footsteps retreating, and after a time he turned back to watch him.

"Come on," Tall Boy said to Ramesh. "We go down there and send them off."

"Very good," Ramesh said, and they scampered to the file of tanks, jabbering all the way.

"You liar," Philips said, sitting again. "Only to build and not to preach!"

A burst of machine-gun fire silenced him; startled, they half rose. "They are just checking their guns," Philips said, and another burst followed, and a third. "I hope Ramesh and Tall Boy keep out of the way."

"Wouldn't do to kill anybody," Morrison said sulenly.

"Oh, shut up," Philips said. "If you really feel that way, go and stop them. There is dynamite at the bridge.

Go blow it up."

"You're out of your mind."

"No, no. Go. Go and do it. If it means so much."

"They'd come in helicopters," Morrison said.

"But then it would not be your fault."

"Oh, go to hell," Morrison said. "I'm no good at this. All I know is I built a bridge and he's my first customer." Another burst of fire, and then a series; eight, Morrison thought, and realized that he had been counting.

"You are a fool." There was anger in Philips's voice, and Morrison's anger rose to answer; but he listened. "Every time you use a telephone, or a car, or push a button anywhere, you are profiting by the death of men. Or that crane, that marvelous crane that Tall Boy loves. Your whole bloody civilization is built on the bones of serfs, slaves, discards. But now that you have it all, you adore the untutored savage and come to me and the major with your wholesome sermons. Oh, the righteous!" He was still angry, his head forward and his small eyes bright; he was like a bear. "You must go to the cinema some time in the capital. Watch one of your war films, or a western, and see what happens when the good man kills the bad man."

"Cheers and hisses," Morrison said.

"No. They laugh. They laugh loudly. But they do not laugh at your rich man's comedies. Oh no. They notice the Rolls-Royce or the little red sports car. They notice the washing machine and the telephone and the piano, and the lift like a French drawing room. And they

are very serious when they see all that. And how would
you like to have your gall bladder out with no anes-
thesia?"

Startled, Morrison swallowed some of his drink and
said, "Not at all. What's that got to do with anything?"

"I am telling you that you live by technology, and you
care not a damn for the men who died perfecting ether.
Were you vaccinated when you came here?"

"Of course."

"There you are then. In the early days three hundred
people died here from vaccinations. One and a half million did not, and are free of the smallpox."

"Oh hell," Morrison exploded. "Your fancy arguments from college. We're talking about *people*.
Friends. People I gave my word to."

"Your word. They never believed you. They would
never believe any white man."

"But they would believe the black man who is going
in there with tanks."

Philips shrugged wearily. He slumped and was no
longer a bear. "You do not know that anything bad will
happen."

"No. It's all right as long as I don't know. I can always apologize later if necessary." His bones ached. He
remembered the morning, and the hot climb up the hill,
and the sun beating down on the granite, and his beautiful bridge in the distance.

"You are like a small boy," Philips said sleepily. "You
live by stories and films and fairy tales. The preachers
tell you that if you do not kill you will not die, and so

forth. You need villains and heroes, and happy endings, or sad endings if they are inspiring enough. So now you want a grand climax. Morrison against a squadron of tanks. Well, there are no grand climaxes. No supreme sacrifices. No floods, fires, or satisfying massacres. There is only a lot of useless misery and death that we have to live with. And work. There is plenty of work to be done, and you cannot hold up the work because you feel rotten about Hiroshima."

"Leave me alone about Hiroshima," Morrison said.

"All right," Philips said. "I will even take that back. But you know, I could tell what you were thinking when you came here. Waiting for. Searching for. Adventure and romance and your heroes and villains. Monkeys and jaguars. Soldiers of fortune and tom-toms. God knows what. But it never happens that way. Heroes pick their noses and villains are kind to old women, and the dashing soldier of fortune has crab lice. Your beautiful carrion crows are only vultures after all, and their real beauty is that they save us from drowning in carrion. But that is not enough for you. You need bedtime stories and pretty pictures. Life is not enough for you because it is too sad and slow, garbled, indecisive. Lepers. Civil servants. Promises broken. Fist fights that peter out— that was no grand climax at Martha's, was it now. Women who are not beautiful and men who are not brave. Your marriage that was no marriage. That was not a tragedy. A sadness, yes. A mistake. But you had to make a tragedy of it, a bedtime story. And the war. I heard you brag that you had killed no one in the war. I have wanted to tell you these things for a long time, you know."

"I wasn't bragging," Morrison said glumly. The soldiers were in their tanks and the major was shouting orders. His voice was higher when he gave orders; a tenor, almost shrill.

"You were, my foolish friend. Saint Moe. No guilt for you. Only the blood-sickness to show yourself how pure you were. Guilt was only for the brutes who killed. Well, you owe them thanks. They lie awake and know they have killed."

"They don't lie awake at all," Morrison said. "They go bowling. They band together and wear funny hats and persecute professors." The lead tank sputtered and roared, and then the others.

"But they killed for you, so you could stay pure in your cell and speculate about right and wrong and come down here and preach. Listen: whatever it is that made man out of turtles also made that war. And built this bridge. And invented ether. And there was killing every step of the way. A million years ago some species of primate probably got killed off that in the end would have been much smarter and nobler than you and I."

"What do you want me to do then?" Morrison tried to sneer but could not. "Go kill somebody so I can belong? Forget about right and wrong and just stomp on anything that interferes with my work?"

"Oh, for God's sake!" Philips sprang to his feet, furious. "You sit there with money in the bank and worry about your conscience and your sex and your salvation, and pretty soon you are thinking of no one but yourself,

and what kind of life is that? Here thousands of people
die stupidly every day, but at least we do not make a way
of life out of moaning and groaning, waiting for a rev-
elation from God or the poets. We have tuberculosis
and riots and blind children and bellies swollen with
starch, and that is the meaning of life to us, that is what
we work on, because we cannot afford the luxury of
righteousness. We need sewers, not bush niggers. And
least of all lords of the world to teach us how to deceive
ourselves and live by pretty pictures! Just keep your
garbage, your elegant and well-fed hypocrisies, and
leave us alone!"

The tanks plunged forward, parallel, and thundered
to the road; from the lead tank the major waved to
them, and Morrison, despising himself, waved back. He
and Philips stepped into the sunlight to watch them go.
The lead tank swung south, and one by one the others
clattered after it. They gleamed and racketed.

Morrison stared after them hopelessly, and his sadness became pain. "Christ, Philips!" he cried. "They
have something! Something we need. They are themselves. With a dignity. They have an innocence!"

"Innocence is another name for ignorance," Philips
said brutally. "You want a private little reservoir of the
primitive, that you can come and dabble your feet in
when the going is rough. The great white father," and
that hurt, and Morrison turned away, "and buy their
baskets for a penny apiece. They can survive as exhibits
or as slaves," Philips said harshly. "Is that what you
want?"

"No," Morrison said. "Is that all? Don't they mean

anything? Even as—as reminders?"

"We need no such reminders," Philips said coldly. "We are not children, to be reminded. And there is more dignity in one full belly, in one cured leper, in one kindergarten, then in all the murderous, superstitious noble savages who ever lived. If you cannot see that, then go home. Just go home. To your country where men cry when a dog dies."

The last tank vanished around the far bend like a ratler's tail.

"And if you remember nothing else," Philips said, "remember what the major said. Because it is the most important thing we have to say to you, and you refuse to listen. All of you," and he said it slowly, as if he were suppressing a shudder, or a blow: "What matters here is not what is done, but that *we* do it."

But Morrison barely heard him, because he had thought of something, and said with new excitement, with a sureness and even a bitter joy, "You're wrong, Philips. I should have done something. Anything. Blown the bridge."

"Go home," Philips said. Ramesh and Tall Boy ambled toward them, chatting and chuckling.

"No," Morrison said with a kind of triumph. "Because one of those women may be carrying my son."

Philips faced him, close and calm, barely contemptuous, and said icily, "Then the chances are one in three that he will be born. Syphilis is endemic in those villages. Did no one tell you that?"

Morrison only gaped; the sun stood still, the earth

stood still, his very blood stood still. Waves of heat battered him, and stopped his breath. Then he was quite
cold. Philips was far off, and the light undulated. "Ah,
God," he said, with sudden fire in his groin, sudden ice,
and his legs trembling. "Ah, God." And then sweat
came, in rivers.

"Greetings," Ramesh said. "My goodness, what a spectacle that was!"

"Lord Jesus," Tall Boy said. "Those machines!"

"You should get out of the sun," Ramesh said to Morrison. "You look dizzy. My, my. And pale."

"Perhaps milord would like a stiff drink." Philips
grinned.

"Just get me to a doctor," Morrison whispered. "Just
get me out of here."

12

"Positive." The doctor was called Kirby and loved a joke. He was round and friendly, with gray hair and black skin, in a white shirt and shorts, and tennis shoes. His hands were sure, and he had trained at St. Thomas's in London. The white-tiled walls blushed a faint yellow in the moist morning light. "Congratulations. You're a father. Millions of bouncing baby spirochetes. The new world's gift to the old."

Positive. Morrison sniffed: alcohol. None of this seemed to matter too much.

"We'll have you right as rain in a week," Doctor Kirby said. "Modern science. You'll never be a Nietzsche. Maupassant. Gauguin."

Morrison sat like a rotting pumpkin.

"Penicillin," the doctor said. "Know what that means? A very very little penis. What you should have had two weeks ago." Mirth erupted.

Morrison said nothing.

"Where did you pick this up? Do you know?"

"In the bush," Morrison said.

"Oh," said the doctor. "Tourist?"

Morrison winced as the needle sank home.

He walked in the capital. His office was perhaps a mile from his hotel. He walked both ways, and watched the sky: wisps of gray and yellow floated south and west, and merged to form small, dirty clouds: more each day, but no rain. The sky itself was hostile and oppressive. His shirt was a nuisance, always wet beneath the arms, sometimes soaked through in back. There seemed to be more dark shirts in the street, and more khaki. The people were quieter and more sullen, and there were more old women with hairy moles, and more cripples. He ate very little, and drank no alcohol. Alcohol was not forbidden but he required, consciously, not sure why, a small mortification of the flesh. And then he was not thinking, his mind had quit, and he shied from stimulation. His lids were always heavy. Isaacson said, "This is the government file. Contracts, bonds, and so forth."

"Yes," Morrison said. "I wish it would rain."

"So do we all. The humidity is maddening. You seem quite worn out, if I may say so."

"Yes," Morrison said. He took a taxi once, twelve miles, to the breakwater and the sea-wall, and he sat for an hour sweltering in the haze, washed now and then by a sluggish, salty puff of air. He saw freighters pass, and a lugger, and he watched convicts in light blue shorts unloading baskets and barrels of fish. The convicts looked like convicts. Cutthroats. Then he rode back to town, and when it was time to pay the driver he stared at the bills in his hand, finding impossible the addition and subtraction of this strange currency. He almost wept at that moment, but even tears were denied him. He shouted at little Gordon one morning. The fried eggs were overcooked and cold and he shouted, "God damn it, Gordon."

"Yes sir," Gordon said, and removed the eggs. Morrison was violently ashamed. In the office he signed his name to assorted certificates, petitions, and quitclaims. He made a small package of his letters from Devoe and the carbon copies of his replies. His photographs proved impressive. He knew they were impressive but was not, himself, impressed. Some evenings he sat on a bench on the mall before his hotel and studied the limp flowers. He knew that he should say farewell to Mother Martha, and knew also that he would not. It had been a pleasure to know one woman to whom he could talk with openness and without defenses, but he knew that he would not go to see her. "Bush niggers," she would say. "With all the nice ladies I got here. Lollie thought you were cute. I wish it would rain." He must remember to settle his bill with Philips. He would keep his accounts straight if nothing else, and would owe no man money. Where I come from that is a sign of character, he thought with bitterness.

Goray said, "Our engineers have inspected the bridge, jumped up and down, kicked the railings, and so forth. They were very pleased. They have asked if I could arrange a dinner and if you would care to lecture."

"Sorry. Philips will do it, and do it well. I'm leaving Sunday."

"So soon? So soon? I did not know. You will miss the ceremonies. But you will be back."

"Of course," he lied politely.

"Then I must buy you a drink." Goray snapped his fingers.

"Coffee, please. What happened to the people across the bridge?"

"We rounded them up and moved them. In the end they will be happier. We gave them the large army tents, with wooden floors, and they have a stream. Or so I hear. A schoolteacher has been assigned to them."

"Oh," Morrison said. "And have you found the border?"

"We are mapping now."

"Since the beginning of time," Morrison said, "that border has not existed. Why should it exist now?"

"Well, we never existed either," Goray said merrily. "And now we do, and we must know who we are, and what we have."

"Of course."

"I wish it would rain," Goray said.

Morrison asked Gordon to help him pack, which was unnecessary, and when the packing was finished he gave Gordon twenty dollars American and they were good friends again. Still a tourist, he thought. Amid all this—splendor and rot, whores and generals, monkeys and jaguars, birth death and fornication—I am the same pulpy blind slug with a white underbelly and traveler's checks. There was a brief shower that night, but his room was air-conditioned, and he scarcely noticed.

He went alone to the airport—Philips was to meet him there—with his one bag, and was silent in the car. He remembered that he had not bought souvenirs. But he

had Ramesh's fan. He saw once more the Indian homes
and the red and white flags, the drainage ditches, the
burnt-out black clearings, the bicyclists and the old men
nodding on carts. It was all vivid and earthy in the
steamy air of noon. One cart was hitched to three donkeys side by side. Approaching the molasses factory,
Morrison took a deep breath, to hold as long as he could,
but then he released it and took in more, and the stench
with it that he would not forget. Perhaps in the end he
would remember only that. His gorge rose but he swallowed it down, and survived. The sun broke through
lowering clouds, and all that he saw was suddenly bright
and sharp. His arms against his white shirt were a deep
brown. That would not last. Carrion crows fell from
the sky and swooped away. They were only vultures. Far
off the jungle was thick and green, and beneath the
green there would be shade and running streams. Men
and women lazed outside the taverns.

Morrison sat limp and moist. He ceased noticing
things and people, and let the heat and the colors sur-
round him and invade him. He thought of nothing, and
moved through the landscape like a part of it, barely
alive.

The car stopped before an unpainted wooden shack.

"Please," the driver said. "This is my sister. I have
a parcel."

Morrison nodded, and the man left the car. Outside
the shack chickens pecked and strutted, keeping to the
shade of the glossy green shrubs. Under one shrub lay a
goat, on his back, legs in the air. Morrison could not re-

call another supine goat. Perhaps it was dead.

Soon they were in the crisscross of roads that announced the airport, and Morrison was melancholy. At
the shed he tipped the driver and allowed a porter to
take his bag. The airport was flat and endless beneath
the dull sky. Morrison presented his ticket. The formali-
ties were brief. He joined several local men on a long
wooden bench, out on the veranda where they could
see the aircraft come and go. The men rose immediately
in servility and distaste, but Morrison said, "Oh sit down.
Too hot to move," and they did sit, after a moment of
indecision. There was no sign of Philips. The only aircraft in sight was an ancient transport, homely and alone
at the far edge of the field, but Morrison heard a stuttering drone and sure enough, there it was, his own,
gleaming silver, settling gently a mile from him. Now I
would like a drink, he thought, as the aircraft droned
closer. A drop of rain spattered to the tarmac before
him, and then another; then more, and more, until in
seconds the ancient transport was masked. "Ah," said
one of the men, and they all said, "Ah." The rain was
arrogant, implacable; undulating sheets of water
seethed and billowed with a hollow rattle. "This the
real thing," one man said. Morrison wondered if he
would leave today after all.

Then the rain ceased, abruptly, and left the field
clean and steaming under a mother-of-pearl sky. His aircraft approached, and stood monstrous and gleaming.

"Hello," Philips said. Morrison turned. There were
silvery beads of rain on Philips's hair, and his red shirt

was damp. Ramesh and Tall Boy stood behind him.

"Hello," Morrison said. "Just in time."

"Good," Philips said. Men in orange slickers rushed out with a gangway. A man without a slicker stood in a puddle bearing furled umbrellas. He squinted up at the sky and returned to the shed.

"Take a seat," Morrison said. The local men were still on the bench, but Philips made shooing motions and clucking sounds, and they lazed away cheerfully.

The four of them sat down and stared out at the pearly sky and the paunchy black clouds. Morrison had nothing much to say. They were good men and so was he in his way, and this farewell at the airport was only more foolishness.

"Why don't we just say good-bye now?" he said. "You can get on back."

"Plenty of time," Philips said.

Ramesh cleared his throat and smiled quickly. "Will you be coming back here?"

"No."

"There is a lot to do," Philips said.

"I know."

"A dam. And bridges, and housing, and more roads."

"Good luck," Morrison said. "My sincere good wishes."

Philips's lips were tight. "All right," he said.

They watched passengers descend. The stewardess smiled and smiled.

"Well, I brought you this here," Tall Boy said. It was a plain index card, unlined. On one side was written, in a clear sloping hand, ABCDEFGHIJKLMNOPQRSTUV WXYZ, and on the other, *abcdefghijklmnopqrstuvw xyz Yours Truly Tall Boy With Thanks.*

It was a relief to smile. Tall Boy also smiled, and saluted off his temple with one unmilitary finger. "I'll keep this," Morrison said. "So I wasn't altogether wasted."

"Oh, stop it," Philips said. "There is so much you could do here."

"Not me," Morrison said. "There's nothing for me to do here."

"You are sulking," Philips said.

"No," Morrison said. "You don't need me."

"This is a mistake," Philips said. "You are running away from something when you ought to be fighting it."

"I can't fight myself," Morrison said.

"What will you do?"

"Go back to my job. Build a shopping center. We'll condemn some Indian land and use only the best redwood. After a while you'll drop a bomb on us and it won't matter."

"Nobody wants to drop bombs," Philips muttered.

"In fifty years we'll only be in the way," Morrison explained modestly.

"Oh hell," Philips said. "There is no talking to you."

"The job was the best I can remember," Ramesh said. "It was a pleasure working with a man we could like."

"You a fine fellow," Tall Boy said, and clapped him on the shoulder with a hand like a hammer.

Philips said nothing, but looked steadily at Morrison.

Then he said, "I have almost no friends. There is no one who uses my first name."

"Problems," Morrison said. "Everybody has problems." Rage played about them both, and Morrison ached. Damn him!

"I have no house and no village," Philips said. "I have read Locke and Marx and I live in a stew of corrupt politicians. I am a slave to goatish lusts. All you can do is grow up. Accept it all and go on building. There is a world to build." He turned away then, as if it had taken him thirty years to learn that and he had only that to say. Yet he started to speak again; and fell silent.

"Count me out," Morrison said, his chest tight. "You got your bridge. I'm going home."

"Not with a bang but a whimper," Philips said.

"That's it."

"All right," Philips said briskly. He rose. "Good-bye. Good luck."

"Good-bye. Good luck." They shook hands, and then Morrison shook hands with Ramesh and Tall Boy, and they all stood there awkwardly for a while like visitors in a hospital.

"Hell," Philips said. "Nobody hurt your niggers."

"That's right," Morrison said. "Nobody hurt my niggers."

Then they went away. They went through the doorway of the shed and were lost in the crowd.

Soon a natty official came onto the veranda to announce Morrison's flight. A fresh fall of rain had begun to spatter the tarmac, and by the time Morrison reached the hole in the side of the aircraft, his hair and shoulders were wet, his face streaming. He took a window seat, starboard, and watched the rain swell and thicken until the wall of distant jungle was lost to sight. Lines of froth raced across the runway like combers. A man in an orange slicker dashed beneath the wing. Morrison was not nervous. Nothing could happen to you if you did not exist. He was not sure who he was, or what, so nothing could happen to him. In time he might make discoveries. Even a new start. Perhaps a new start was possible. Perhaps he could find his own borders and clear them and map them. A man was not nothing until he was dead. Morrison was not dead. That much he could say for himself. In time his eyes would uncross, and he would grasp his own toes and gurgle, and his smile would mean more than gas.

His arms were solid and very brown against his white shirt. His arms were his vanity. He examined the hairs. They had been reddish when he was pale but now they were golden.

Soon the engines whined, and he fastened his belt, and the aircraft lumbered forward. At the head of the runway they turned, and for a moment he could see the wooden shed with the wet flag hanging limp, and then the rain washed it out, great silver sheets of rain, and they had to wait twenty minutes. That was no bother to Morrison except for the man beside him. The man was a compatriot, beefy, with a large jaw and a small, thoroughly veined nose, and a tendency to talk. A Pittsburgher, he said. To a silent Morrison he went on about one thing and another while they waited; chiefly what a filthy and primitive country this was, and what filthy and primitive people lived in it. When the rain diminished and they lunged into that terrific first surge, he announced his name and held forth a chummy hand. Morrison smiled like Bawi because he felt rotten, very rotten, exceptionally rotten just then, and a first step was necessary, some first step, you see, so he grinned that broad toothy grin and rolled his eyes dementedly and boomed, "Yis sor! Vairy fuckin hallo!" and he completed his long voyage in a decent and honorable solitude.